THE PARASITE

BY

NEAL ASHER

First published 1996 by Tanjen LTD.

This edition published by Neal Asher on
Amazon Kindle.

Prologue

Space watched with its glinting spider eyes as the great tri-clawed link miner poised in the emptiness like a grasping robotic hand. Star-shine glimmered like oil on its pitted hull whilst inside its single occupant waited, impatiently.

'I have no reading as yet,' said Jack as he rubbed a hand over his stubbled cheek. He could have shaved but felt the stubble necessary to reinforce his persona as a rugged old hand.

Before him, above the touch console, the screen displayed the menace of emptiness and the distant toy-like shape of Saturn. Two minutes passed before he spoke again.

'I have it now, it's half a million miles out and closing. Should be here in about three hours. I think it's time to go for initial boost.'

He shifted the view of the screen to the area of space above Orion's belt. Three hours. He again checked the comet's position and relative speed on the laser-bounce detector, swore quietly, then allowed the computer to give him a vector. The predicted figures were wrong. The comet was doing half again its previously estimated fall speed, so with a relished vehemence he told the ship's log about the mistake. It was unnecessary to do so, since the figures were recorded and simultaneously transmitted to TCC, but it made him feel better to spit out some bile.

Eighty thousand tons of complex ices and rock hurtled through void, satellite fragments swirling about it, each with the destructive potential of an armour-piercing shell. Jack tapped the enable touch-plate with his forefinger then looked yearningly at Ignition Ten as the clock connected to the heating elements of the main boosters started its slow countdown. The link miner glinted blue stars of manoeuvring jets and slowly turned its tri-claw to the as yet invisible hammer of ice and rock. Jack's mouth was dry.

Once, apparently, the ionic boosters of a link miner had failed to shut down during an interception like this. The brief flash was witnessed by astronomers in the northern hemisphere of Earth and when, seven months later, the comet had swung round the sun on an altered parabola, its coma had been a weird ethereal blue before it splashed on Venus's atmosphere in spectacular galvanic death. It is said that one twisted claw of the link miner now orbits that planet like a reminder of fallibility and hubris – like the floating remains of a crab left by the passing snap of a bass. Jack felt a frisson of fear and shivered as he thought of that relic. Later there would be no time for such superfluous emotions.

Twenty, nineteen ... eighteen ... The display seemed to change with teasing slowness as if spiralling down into stasis; one, but never zero. Still the comet lay out of sight, but if it had been visible it would have been too late. Not that he could not get out of the way in time, but the flare from the ionic boosters would have wrecked the complex ices he had come here to mine; raising them above the temperature of a hundred and fifty degrees Kelvin to their flare point where they would have become normal 'dirty' water ices. He pushed his head back into the padded brace and made sure he was well back in the form-fitting chair.

Three ... two ... one ... The display flickered and he tapped Ignition Ten – so called because of the highest g-force it could boost to, but one he did not need now. Then he prepared himself for the hour of high-gee needed at his present vector needed to bring him to the intercept point.

From the three junctures of the link miner's talons, miniature suns ignited and flares of ionized water spewed into space. In a minute his ship was at five hundred miles an hour, then a thousand, yet the surrounding stars moved not at all. The acceleration clamped Jack back in his seat, his suit tightening against his body automatically. There was no discomfort at first. It was exhilarating. The discomfort would come later, after perhaps twenty minutes at this acceleration.

On the arm of his chair the ready light came on as basic control transferred to there from the main board. With a finger weighing as much a brick Jack tapped the control that centred up the laser approach display. The comet was still too far away to be seen, but close enough for him to get a more accurate reading from the laser bounce-back. He did a quick mental calculation as the figures came up for him. There was a discrepancy, not outside parameters, but not nice. He calculated, and the computer confirmed, that when the link miner impacted the comet, he would experience an extra six gees of acceleration. The ship could take it but he knew he would black out. Dare he feed more energy into the boost? He dared not. There were millions of Ecu worth of complex ice to be mined and extra energy fed into the boost now might cut that figure by half. He set the automatics on the grab and readied himself as best he could for the impact, which was fifty minutes away now.

Time, as it is wont to do in moments of tension, dragged its leaden feet. In that time Jack enumerated, in order of probability, the many things that could go wrong, starting with burst blood vessels in his brain and finishing with stress fractures at any one of a million points on the ship. Yet, in the last moments when the comet came, he could not help watch with morbid fascination as it grew on the screen. And in those moments it seemed to come so fast. There was a growing blur of grey and white, stars occluded by a growing storm, followed by an explosion of sound. It seemed to Jack he could not survive this. Then the blood drained from his head like wine from a punctured gourd, and let in the blackness.

Chapter One

On waking Jack wanted to vomit, but he bit back on it and the impulse faded. Acceleration had passed now, yet he felt it had not, because of the gentle, almost subliminal, pull of the comet his ship now clung to like a great tick. There were sounds now, transmitted through the leviathan talons of the link miner's claw, the uneasy creaking and static crackling of the ice. He checked the screens and saw two of the talons firmly imbedded. The third had come down across a slab of rock, shattering the slab in the process. The tip of the arm was buried in the ice beyond. It would do.

'Down and held,' he said, more for his own benefit than the log's, then began to free himself from his chair. A glance at another screen showed him that the bore was already eating its way in and that the hold was a quarter full. He had time now to take a look – he always felt a bit superfluous when the automatics took over.

From the life-support blister Jack towed himself down the corridor leading to the loading shaft. There he donned his carbon sixty cold-suit and then clad like a Samurai opened the door to the cold lock, then the door to the deep cold of the loading shaft, ice crystals falling about him in a nacreous snow.

The loading shaft was the bell-shaped underside of the ship, positioned down against the comet at the juncture of the claw's talons below the hold and then living quarters; the mouth of the tick. A hundred feet below him the face of the comet glinted weird colours in the subdued neon. Down the centre of the shaft a twenty-foot diameter pipe revolved slowly as it cut huge plugs of ice from the comet and transferred them to the hold above. Jack tugged on a rung and hauled himself up to the hatch leading into the hold. In a moment he was inside, above the bore and watching as automatics mindlessly sheared the perpetually growing cylinder of ice into coin-like sections which the auto-handlers stacked. There was no sound, just a steady vibration he picked up every time he touched a surface. He moved on into the stacks, like a worshipper moving into the temple of Karnak, surrounded on all sides by pillars of ice shot through with random fluorescence. All looked well until he reached the back of the hold.

Something ... something in the ice.

It was a flaw, twenty feet long and spiralling up a nearby pillar, disjointed where the shear had cut the blocks. He swore, because the automatics should have picked up on contaminants like this. Noting the number – J12 – he made a mental note to have this stack transferred for fuel, then reached out to touch the flaw.

Something ... fibrous?

His glove came away with a substance like candy floss sticking to it. Immediately he felt intense cold in his fingers. Shit! He propelled himself as fast he could to the nearest cold lock. By the time the lock opened to his command he had lost the feeling in three of his fingers and ice burn was creeping into his hand. In the cold lock his suit frosted a millimetre thick with ice, then beaded with water. Fumbling, he removed his helmet and air pack, insulated body armour and boots. The gloves always came off last as a precaution against cold burn from the suit. His right glove had something viscous on it. He dropped it to the floor and it shattered. It should not have. A glance at his hand confirmed his fears. He would lose three of his fingers and part of his hand. His hand ached from cold burn and his fingers were numb, and suddenly he felt very ill. He vomited, then staggered back to his living quarters.

In fifteen hours both the hold and water tank of the link miner were full. Trying to ignore the horrible ache in his hand and the deadness of his fingers, now clad in a thick glove he had not yet dared to take off, Jack strapped himself in his acceleration chair and keyed the automatics that would release the link miner from the comet. Normally he would have done this with the manual controls, but he felt ill, he had the shakes, his eyes were streaming with their whites all but gone in a red web-work, and every minute or so he sneezed, when his coughing allowed it. He knew what this was: extreme allergic reaction. He had taken antihistamines but they did not seem to be doing any good.

The automatics blew the three talons of the claw free then threw the link miner from the comet in a cloud of vapour and glittering shards of ice, turned it, and a blast from the ion drive put it on a new course. Main deceleration would be nearer to the satellite factories in near Earth orbit. Jack sat still and stared at the receding comet, his expression hard, then he focused his attention on the communicator. He should really transmit; tell them back at TCC what had happened, but he was reluctant. One whiff of this and there would be quarantine for him and restrictions on this load of ice. Too much money was at stake. Having bought into the expedition with credit from his coming redundancy payment, ten per cent of The Cryon Corporation profits would go to him. Thereafter there would be no more chances since comet mining was being phased out, it being made obsolete by satellite industry. He gazed at his hand. An accident; a loose seal on a glove. So unfortunate that the glove had been dropped in the central shaft and remained on the comet…

There was no other evidence. The contaminated ice had been converted to water and used in the boost away from the comet. His word should be sufficient. He sneezed then coughed. All he had to do now was get rid of this damned reaction. He deliberately turned from the communicator and peered up at the screens.

'Out and away,' he said, throwing words into the void. He felt fuzzy headed, but it would pass. He pushed his undamaged hand up his stubbled face and back across his hair, and felt a stickiness there. Studying his hand he saw blood on his palm. He reached up to the side of his head and probed, fingertips coming away bloody. He was bleeding from his ears. Allergic reaction. That was all.

Five days after he should have gone into hibernation sleep the allergic reaction had diminished somewhat, but the med-scanner diagnosed gangrene in his hand. He knew that if he was to save at least part of it he would have to operate on it himself. Yet, when the time came, with his hand as dead as a sand filled glove, he could not make the first cut with the laser scalpel. This was not uncommon. The situation had occurred before on long flights. After a time he taped his hand up and pulled a polythene glove over it to contain the smell. Then, with a weary reluctance, he made his way to the plastic coffin where he would sleep away the next two years. He would think of something when he woke. He had to.

Horribly bright light shone through his eyelids showing a tracery of veins like rivers on an incarnadine map. A persistent buzzing filled his ears as of an alarm clock without a snooze button. Jack attempted to swear but found the effort too much. He slept.

The second waking was always easier though never remembered as such. Jack opened his eyes to the gleaming arc of the lid above him as it revolved aside. He unzipped the restraining bag from the inside then he reached for the tubes that had been plugged into a carotid artery and jugular vein. A light tug and they came away leaving bloodless wounds that had been sealed days previously. He then reached to pull himself from the coffin. This was the bit he really hated: the cold, and the gnawing hunger that could not be immediately satisfied because he felt so sick. The nausea was the understandable reaction of his body to the antifreeze it had contained. The substance might well have been quite normal for a certain weird Russian rodent, but he was human. As his hand came down on the cold edge he sneezed, and remembered.

Even as he coughed and sneezed his way to the control chair, Jack was surprised at how quickly the nausea receded and just how much he could eat only minutes after thaw-up, yet, he still felt as if his proper place was back in the coffin. It took an extreme act of will thereafter for him to turn on the screens, the computer, and the radio. From them he quickly learnt that he was days yet from home. Then he noticed that the finger he had stabbed at the touch plates was one of the ones he should have amputated. He peeled off the polythene glove, then the tape, which came away with a thick layer of dead skin, and stared at his fingers for a long time, before sneezing then slumping back in his seat.

The Cryon corporation station was a cylinder a mile long and half a mile wide, studded with the excrescences of lounges, high-grav gyms, instrument pods and docking tubes, and had shuttles clinging to it like wasps on an apple core. As soon as it came into view over Earth's sapphire horizon, Jack allowed his radio to spring into raucous life.

'This is TCC calling link miner Zero, do you hear this Jack? ... Come on, answer.'

Jack shook himself. He felt as dry and heavy as new-cast lead and had a thirst that would not go away. How long had he been sitting here with the radio going?

'Here,' he said, begrudgingly.

'Thank Christ! You took your time replying. There's a correct way to do these things ... are you okay?'

Okay? For a moment he could not make sense of that. His thoughts were sluggish and dull. He groped for an excuse. 'Usual shit – ice condensed round the aerial.'

'You should have cleared that just after leaving the comet.'

Jack was suddenly, almost convulsively aware of danger. He would become subject to close scrutiny if he did not give plausible responses, and could end up in trouble very quickly. Suddenly he was thinking with unaccustomed clarity.

'What does it matter? I'm here now. Do you think I'd fool around with this shipment? I've got to think of my percentage.'

In the background a sharp exchange ensued, shortly followed by a reluctant reply. 'Okay Jack, bring her in. We'll take her on automatics at five hundred meters.'

'You will not,' said Jack, sitting upright. 'I'll bring her in myself.'

Why did he say that? He had not docked on manual in years. Did he fear the automatics that much?

'No ... sorry ... yeah,' he quickly corrected. 'Take her at five hundred.'

When the automatics took over, Jack dug his fingers into the arms of his chair, his body as rigid as a plank. He was scared, but just could not think why. There had been no docking accidents in years and there were none this time.

The doctor scraped at the dead skin to reveal new pink skin underneath, examined that in puzzlement then abruptly dropped his scalpel in the sterilization tray. Jack waited for comment as the doctor removed his surgical gloves, but the man continued to peer at the dry, seemingly mummified fingers.

'Okay?' Jack asked.

The doctor nodded. 'Just dead skin.'

'I can go then?'

The doctor dumped his gloves in a bin and went on, 'It healed remarkably quickly and I'm surprised there was no necrosis. You were lucky. Most cold suit breaches normally result in the loss of something, up to and including life.'

'Yeah,' said Jack, angry at the suspicion in the doctor's voice, and having to put heavy restraint on an abrupt urge to violence. So, he had healed quickly, what was wrong with that?

'Clean bill of health then?' Jack commented, wondering why he felt so guilty.

'For now, though I'd like to do a full scan later when you have the time.' The doctor gazed at him in perplexity. 'There are still some other symptoms to be accounted for.'

'Yeah, when I have the time.'

The doctor continued gazing at him, then casually added, 'Your on-board med-scanner diagnosed gangrene.'

Had it?

'Time that ship was thoroughly checked out,' said Jack. 'Faulty cold suits and faulty med-scanners make for dead pilots and profitless trips, both of which are of great concern to me.' He stood up and stepped away from the chair, poised, his healing fingers clenching into a fist.

I'll have to kill him.

The doctor nodded and turned away. 'Come back when you can.' He seemed stiff-backed as he walked away.

When I can. I could break his neck now. Why? Why?

Jack backed to the door flushed with panic. He did not want inspections, but murder? In a moment he was outside the door, breathing heavily, a sick feeling in the pit of his stomach and rage coiled at the base of his spine. He wanted to take his money and run, get back to Earth, normality, away from this aseptic environment. He did not want to kill. What purpose was served by killing?

Calm took its time returning to him.

The delta-wing re-entry shuttle detached from the TCC station and fell like a sycamore seed in an arc over the jewel of Earth. Retro rockets flared and it stabilized level with Earth's horizon, leaving the station turning against the stars like a lapidary's barrel for polishing asteroids. Then the main engine glared and it sped for that horizon.

Strapped into the plush white leather of an acceleration chair, Jack breathed a sigh of relief and clutched his case to his lap. There had been so many things he had needed to check, but they were an excuse for his paranoiac horror of a full med-scan. He had demanded release and they had not refused, but there had been delays in the transference of credit to his Ecubank account. However, aboard the station credit had been readily available to him, just as had been the black market in satellite-grown memory crystals.

Doctor Bannerman supped coffee from his capped mug and opened his medical journal with weary disinterest. He had other things on his mind. Twice now he had been put off and he was getting angry. Smith's fingers should not have healed like that, no way. The man had suffered some kind of allergic reaction as well, and just on that evidence alone Bannerman had requested quarantine, and been refused. When he had seen the fuzzy tape from the med-scanner he had requested it again, and urgently. He shook his head. It made him feel cold inside when he considered what he had seen there. Yet, damn them, they had refused again. And he knew why.

Money.

That was what this was all about. Had they accepted his judgement on Jack Smith the same quarantine order would have applied to the ship and its cargo: millions of ecu worth of complex ices. He gazed up from his journal and through the window of the lounge, which showed the curve of the TCC station seeming curving up to the blue-white expanse of Earth, which was now sinking as the lounge he occupied spun away from it. On that curve, like an insect on the flank of some huge metallic buffalo, he could see the link miner docked at the mouth of a loading bay with activity around it – the motes of light that were auto-handler drays. They were unloading the ship as quickly as possible. He suspected it would go for breaking rather quickly too.

Money.

The corporation could lose a huge percentage of their profit. The prices of mined comet ice had been dropping for some time, ever since it had been possible to duplicate, in satellite factories, the processes the ice had previously undergone in the Oort Cloud. *I've done my job*, Bannerman told himself, and he flicked through his journal without seeing, and drank his coffee without tasting.

Damn the mercenary bastards.

It was no good. He had done his job, but he had not done all he could. He was a doctor; he had responsibilities. And he had other masters. Abruptly he stood up, rising ridiculously high out of his seat in the low spin gravity of the station. When his Velcro soles touched the carpet again he headed for the door. It might cost him his job, but somebody had to be informed.

The transmitter lay on the table in his cabin disguised as a hand diagnosticer. It had the letters imprinted in its plastic W.H.O. like a question, and had in fact been manufactured by World Health. Bannerman sat down and the chair back automatically folded round him. With care he pushed a concealed switch on the side of the diagnosticer and flicked up the touch panel to reveal a second panel of lettered buttons underneath. He typed out his message:

LINK MINER ONE HAS BEEN IN CONTACT WITH AN ETO. PILOT JACK SMITH CARRYING PARASITIC ORGANISM. REQUEST FOR QUARANTINE REFUSED BY TCC. SMITH NOT RETURNED FOR MEDSCAN. BELIEVE FINANCIAL-

There was a hammering at his door. His fingers hesitated over the buttons and he felt a trickle of sweat run down his backbone.

Here it comes.

He finished the message.

-MOTIVATION.

The door burst open. He hit transmit, just before an arm reached over his shoulder and snatched up the diagnosticer. He turned as it bounced on the floor.

'What the hell do you think you're doing?'

A heel came down on the instrument, smashing it to fragments that bounced across the carpet in slow motion. Bannerman gaped at it, then looked up. A man and a woman stood in the room, both of them dressed in dark grey TCC businesswear, both of them with cropped blond hair, both of them expressionless. The woman spoke.

‘Doctor Bannerman, the Chairman will see you now.’

Bannerman remained in his seat. He did not like this.

‘What’s the point? The ice is being unloaded. Smith has not returned for his med-scan. The Chairman has no intention of allowing quarantine. I’ll just stay here if you don’t mind.’

‘You will come with us.’

Simultaneously they took hold of him and dragged him to his feet.

‘You have no right to do this!’ Bannerman shouted, hoping someone else would hear, then he fell silent as something hard stabbed against his belly. He gazed down to see a small matt pistol the woman held.

‘You will come with us.’

He complied.

They led him from his cabin, down the aseptic corridors of the medical quarter then to the tastefully panelled corridors of the executive quarter and to a lift with plush upholstered bench seats. They thrust him inside and stepped back. The doors slammed shut and the lift jerked up against the spin of the station.

The lift was taking him to the Chairman’s office, which wasn’t so bad. He closed his eyes for a moment and breathed more easily. When the doors slid open he saw he was right, only separated him from the office itself stood a Perspex screen, beyond which a corpulent figure slouched in an armchair in a shadowed room.

‘Doctor Bannerman,’ said Geoffrey Haven, Chairman of The Cryon Corporation and a tantamount dictator up here. He was called the Toad by those who dared, but not many did dare.

'What is the meaning of this?' Bannerman asked, realizing he had been speaking in clichés for the last half hour.

'Life or death,' said the Toad.

Bannerman felt himself go rigid.

The Toad went on, 'You see, I don't like traitors and blabbermouths, especially if they come near to losing me money. What message did you send?'

'I—'

The Toad interrupted, 'No matter. I'll know soon enough and, either way, I'll do what I must. You see, in two minutes I am going to open that lift to a jettison shaft, to vacuum. In the bench seat behind you is a space suit. The record for getting fully suited is fifty-three seconds, so I am giving you plenty of time. You will note the display on the wall is already counting.'

'You can't!' But Bannerman knew he could.

The Toad began to laugh.

Bannerman desperately pulled up the lids on all the seats, found the suit, ripped off his jacket and kicked off his shoes. Twenty seconds. He slid himself into the suit and methodically went through the sealing procedures. Easy. Easy. He pulled on the gauntlets. Forty seconds. He hitched on the air pack and connected it to the helmet. He was going to make it. Fifty seconds. Laughter. That laughter. Something was hissing, then roaring. A door into night opened behind him and an invisible hand snatched him through. As the air gusted from his lungs and his ear drums burst he saw that the display read fifty-three seconds.

The Toad had lied.

Bannerman fell into a vast well, struck its side as he spiralled down.

I can survive. I can survive.

He knew it was possible to live for minutes in vacuum. He reached for the helmet yet it stayed tauntingly out of reach. He saw stars and the Earth like a vast jewel with vision blurring as the moisture evaporated from his eyes which were swelling in their sockets. Then he managed to grab the helmet. Somehow he got it over his head and began to dog it down. The need to breath was unbearable and he could feel blood vessels bursting in his skin. The last dog clicked into place. The safety light glowed a beautiful green and he waited for sweet air to gust from the pack.

There was none.

Chapter Two

Gene looked down at the man sprawled on the bed and wondered if she was doing the right thing staying with him, despite the potential reward. He looked wasted, an atomy. He had told her he did not have one of the new versions of AIDS but had refused to take a med-scan. Gene made sure her shots were up to date.

With annoyance she dumped her acquisitions from the market on the kitchenette floor, turned on the coffee maker and lit up a Moroccan Gold. The smoke calmed her as she waited for him to stir. From the open window came the sounds of Sao Paulo awake: the continual roar of traffic, screeching of brakes, bellowing of air horns and sirens, the mutter and shout of eight million people. The flat was uncomfortably hot, the air thickened and tainted by the fumes from the streets below since hydrogen powered air-cars had yet to make their mark here as they had in Europe.

Jack woke with a spastic jerk then stared up from the bed with bloodshot eyes.

'You're back' he said, and scrubbed at the scum on his lips.

Gene repressed her sarcasm, knowing it would have been wasted at this time in the morning, for his mind would be on only one thing.

'Did you get the food?'

She nodded and lifted a bag up onto the counter separating the kitchen from the main room. Jack came off the bed like a piece of spring steel and was opening the bag before she even had time to release it. He sure didn't move like a man who was ill.

'Carlson said he would look at the merchandise today,' she said.

Jack nodded and dry gulped a handful of vitamin and glucose tablets. Gene wondered if he was on drugs, but had never seen him taking any.

'What is this merchandise?' she asked.

Jack stepped round into the kitchenette and began to break eggs into a pint jug. This was his usual breakfast. He would be hungry again in a couple of hours then a couple of hours after that, then again and again until he went to bed and slept for ten to twelve hours. He ate more in a day than Gene ate in a week, yet he was painfully thin.

'It's not drugs,' he said.

Gene watched him. 'You don't trust me.'

'Where did you say he wanted to meet me?'

'The Cicero, this evening at ten o'clock.'

He nodded and Gene turned away as he gulped down the glutinous mass. Carlson had told her to stick with him and find out where he kept this 'merchandise', though he had not told her what it was. She found this difficult at times since Jack was not easy to live with. With a degree of repressed irritation she stubbed out her joint in the sink and stepped from the kitchenette to the bedroom. There she sprawled herself on the bed with her legs pointing towards the counter where Jack was now mixing a glucose drink. A cloud of dust settled around her. The bed always seemed to be dusty no matter how often she vacuumed it out. Jack seemed to shed skin like a snake and his complexion was always pale no matter how long he spent in the sun. She waved a hand in front of her face then, irritated that he wasn't paying attention, she lifted one leg to show the tops of her stockings and her knickers and began to rub her hand up and down her inner thigh.

'Come on Jack, I feel horny.'

He peered at her as if he did not understand what she meant, then drained a pint of glucose syrup. Gene began to undo the studs of her leather waistcoat. She was very attractive and had a good body. She knew this. This was why Carlson had chosen her all those years ago. Yet with Jack she never knew where she stood. Sometimes he reacted like a sex-starved adolescent, other times he showed no reaction at all. After a moment he grinned a death's head grin then came in from the kitchenette, knelt between her legs, and began to assist her with the waistcoat.

'If it's not drugs then what is it that would interest Carlson?' she asked as she pulled his head down to her breasts.

'I guess it doesn't matter that you know,' he said, his voice muffled as she moaned theatrically in response. 'I have a batch of TCC memory crystals for sale. I sold him one about six months ago when I first returned.' As a reward for that she reached down and began to stroke his penis. His breathing was heavy. This she could handle. This she knew.

'Worth a lot of money. I hope you've got them safe?'

'Safe as safe can be,' he said, using precisely the same accent as the actor in the holovision commercial.

Gene smiled and thought to herself, *in the bank*, then moaned again as he pushed her micro skirt up off her hips, tugged her knickers aside and entered her. Then, being the consummate actress she was, she showed not a hint of the bored resignation she felt as she waited for him to finish.

The security camera followed Jack's progress across the foyer with cyclopean suspicion. No doubt the security guard thought him an unlikely candidate for the custom of Ecubank. He was skeletally thin, had the fevered appearance of a junky, and the jeans and T-shirt that hung on him looked suspiciously as if they might be dirty, not just fashionably scruffy. He probably smelled.

He came, at length, to one of the many service points and rested his hands on the shelf before the armoured glass. The girl behind the glass had difficulty forcing her 'I am waiting to serve you' smile.

'I've come to collect something from my box,' he said.

'Please speak the number of your box into the microphone to your right.'

Jack did as instructed as the girl, Cherry Lane her badge named her, peered at a screen to one side.

'Could you now place your right hand on the touch pad and look into the retinal scanner with your right eye.'

He placed his hand on a matt square on the shelf before him and stared into the green glare of the scanner set in the armoured glass. After a moment a chip card poked out of the shelf at him like a robotic tongue. He yanked it out and left the machine mute.

'Thank you and good evening,' said Cherry Lane.

Jack headed to the door on one side of the foyer, ran the card through a reader, then entered as the door clicked open. The plain box of a room contained a table and chair bolted down in the middle of the floor and a hatch set in the wall opposite. *Two hamburgers please*, thought Jack, and abruptly felt hungry again. He hurried to the hatch, shoved his card into the slot beside. Minutes later he was back in the street clutching his case of memory crystals.

The street was chaos: stall holders out-shouting each other for attention, queues outside the hypermarkets, psychotic drivers in rusting, petrol-driven hulks blaring their horns seemingly without purpose and driving at any pedestrian with the temerity to step from the pavements, which many were frequently forced to do. Jack loved the crowding and he did not know why. Before his trip out to the comet he had hated cities and had always breathed easier upon returning to his house on the edge of the East Anglian flood plain. Here though, he felt a strange, almost sexual, joy.

A hundred yards from the bank he stopped at a snack bar and bought himself a large doner kebab, which he consumed with mechanical efficiency as he checked out his surroundings. A short distance away from him two big thickset Vietnamese men clad in paperwear overalls turned to a African street vendor wearing a ridiculous Chinese hat and began to inspect the cheap jewellery he was selling. Jack finished his kebab, wiped lamb grease on his jeans, picked up his case and moved on. Shortly he stopped at a vending machine and bought a couple of chocolate bars, which he ate with the same mechanical efficiency as the kebab. Behind him the two men were taking a vast interest in a display of women's underwear. Jack felt something feral uncoil inside him and it terrified him more than the knowledge that he was being followed. Jack moved on.

They came at him as he neared his apartment and as the neon and holographic displays were coming on. He felt as tense as a spring and found he could distinguish the sound of their footsteps from the melee of other sounds, and could hear them as they speeded up. To his right lay dark alleyways into one of which, he decided, they intended to force him. Immediately he broke into a run, intending to head where the crowds were thickest, yet, that something inside him seemed to look to where he could flee most easily, where there was least obstruction, and without volition he turned into one of the alleys and sprinted.

No, dammit! No! But he could not stop. He knew, with sickening dread, that this alleyway came to a dead end, but just ran faster.

The alley snaked between windowless buildings that clutched skeletal fire escapes high above. It was littered with piles of decaying refuse from overturned dustbins, and the broken plastic and glass of obsolete computers. Jack soon reached the alley's end where an ancient Citroen quietly rusted. There was no way through, for just beyond the car rose a cliff of slimed brick. He turned, and his fear slid away to be replaced by a sudden anger.

Something is pressing my buttons.

Yet he could not get past the anger. With a shaking hand he placed his case on the bonnet of the Citroen, then turned to meet his pursuers.

They came round the corner at a steady loping jog, aware that he had nowhere to run. One of them held an antique revolver, the other the transparent glitter of a chain-glass flick knife.

Why were they hesitating? Why were they so slow?

Jack advanced and kicked the gunman in the groin and, before that one had even bowed over, struck the other one three times with the edge of his hand. The second man's flesh felt like cotton wool, and Jack could feel bones breaking like bread sticks. He flicked back to the gunman, who was now at last bowed over, and brought his knee up into the man's face to send him reeling back, the revolver arcing through the air.

Slow motion?

For a moment he could not comprehend what was happening, but then realized that it was not them, it was him. He was moving with unhuman speed.

The two men fell simultaneously. Jack stood perfectly still for a moment, then stamped on the one he had kneed. The man's chest collapsed like a blown-up paper bag and lung tissue jetted from his mouth. Jack turned to the other, but saw he presented no danger. This one lay crumpled with his head twisted at an unnatural angle. Jack felt something coil up inside him, as insidious and venomous as a cobra concealing itself under a stone. Abruptly he felt weak and very hungry, but he also felt a sudden need to try and tidy up the mess he had made. He dragged the bodies over to the Citroen and arranged them neatly inside before leaving the alley and heading off to find a food vendor.

A sudden sickening fear choked Gene as she heard a key click into the front door of the flat. Something was wrong; no one should be coming here. *Carlson has sent his men for me. I'm dead.* She put her hand inside her carryall and gripped the comforting solidity of her Taser as the door opened.

Jack?

Jack scrutinized the clothes on the bed, the carryall, and the suitcase.

'You didn't expect me back, did you?'

Gene licked her lips. There was something about him, about his stance and the rapid, almost birdlike movements of his head. She watched him carefully as he placed his case on the coffee table by the wall. They had failed. Somehow Carlson's two killers had failed. She eased the Taser from her carryall and kept it from view.

'I've had it, Jack. I'm leaving.'

He flicked a glance at her then rubbed his hand up his arm as if he were cold. Gene saw the blood on that hand and crusted under his fingernails.

‘You’ve always worked for Carlson,’ he said. ‘I was ill when I sold him that first memory crystal ... didn’t really know what I was doing ... you latched onto me shortly after.’

Gene lifted the Taser and fircd. She was a good shot, and the darts should have taken him in the middle of his chest. His hand blurred as he snatched the darts out of the air, then he was still, the two wires trailing from his hand and hair-thin blue lightning crackling up his arm. Gene glanced down in panic at the Taser’s meter, seeing he had taken a full charge. Then, in an eye-blink he was right up by her, ripping the Taser from her hand and smashing it to fragments against the wall. Next he slammed her down on the floor, knocked the breath out of her, pinning her and speaking in a horribly intense voice.

‘No. ... No. ... No. ...’

The hand round her neck closed like an iron clamp, choking her. She struggled against him but he seemed wholly made of stone. Then abruptly the grip eased.

‘You came very close to dying then.’

He stood up and moved away from her. Gasping and rubbing at her throat she sat upright.

‘What ... now?’ she managed.

Jack had reached the kitchenette by the time she was on her feet.

‘You will go to Carlson,’ he said. ‘You will tell him I will meet him at the agreed time in the Cicero. Tell him I have nineteen more T-storage TCC memory crystals for sale for which I want twenty-five thousand Ecu each or the equivalent in Dollars, Marks, or United African Shillings.’

Gene moved unsteadily to her carryall, threw in the rest of her belongings, grabbed up her suitcase and headed for the door. Like an automaton, Jack broke eggs into a jug. When she reached the door, he looked up. ‘He knows that this is a very good price and one he can make a very great profit on. Tell him also that if he tries to have me killed or the crystals stolen, I will kill him. If he does not believe that, then tell him he will find his men in the alley opposite the computer hypermarket on Magdalene Street.'

Gene believed. At the door shc said, 'They say that cybernetic augmentation is the latest thing out of Osaka. Is that what you have?'

'Yes, if you like,' he said, and gulped eggs.

The Cicero was one of those cellar bars where criminals gathered like rats in a grain store. A flickering neon sign with a downward pointing arrow showed its location, and the hugely fat Chinaman with a shaven head and rat-tail moustache, who sat on a stool by the door, demonstrated that it had a certain seedy exclusivity. As Jack approached, the Chinaman rose to his feet with the silk of his galabia clinging to his rolls of fat.

'I'm expected.'

'Know you?' wondered the Chinaman, tilting his head.

'Jack Smith. I'm here to see Carlson.'

The Chinaman picked up his stool and moved to one side. Jack stepped through the door as that visceral something twitched inside him. He was not fully in control. He knew he was walking on the edge of a razor.

Stairs led down into a huge dimly-lit room redolent of stale drink and hashish smoke, and vibrating to the monotonous thump of dub. Under the tube lights Jack peered through the crowds until he detected Carlson, who sat at a table by the wall with four of his men, and Gene, who sat on his lap with his hand inside her shirt. As Jack advanced to the table Gene spotted him, and whispered in Carlson's ear.

Unlike his men, Carlson did not look the part he played. He was a thin, dapper little man with a tendency to wear suits in pale pastel colours. He was dark-skinned, yet dyed his hair blonde. A single jewelled ring glinted in his nostril. Jack edged warily past a Rasta who was stamping in erratic circles and communing with his god through a cannabis prayer stick, and crossed the room.

'Jack Smith, have a seat.'

Carlson nodded to one of the thugs, who heaved himself reluctantly to his feet and held out his chair for Jack. Jack stared at the man until he backed away, then he sat down placing his case on the table before him. Carlson shoved Gene from his lap and leaned forwards. She rested nervously back against the wall, sneezed, and then coughed. Jack noted her bloodshot eyes then was riveted by the smear of blood on her ear lobe. Abruptly he returned his attention back to Carlson. He did not want to think about what such symptoms might mean.

'The merchandise,' said Carlson with relish, then he studied Jack calculatingly. 'We found Julio and his brother.'

Expressionlessly Jack undid the case, exposed the crystal cubes in their packing, and turned it towards Carlson, who continued to watch Jack for a moment before reaching out to remove one of the cubes.

'How did you come by these?'

Jack shrugged. 'I used to pilot a link miner for TCC.'

Carlson nodded and took an expensive personal unit from his breast pocket. He placed it on the table, opening it out like a wallet, then pressed the cube into the receiver. It flickered. He pressed a couple of touch plates and viewed the display.

'Ten terabytes, finest resolution. I am impressed. The first you brought me was only one terabyte...' He peered at Jack again. 'Twenty-five thousand each you say?'

'A good price and you know it,' said Jack.

Carlson greedily eyed the case then abruptly snapped his fingers. The thug who had given up his chair came to the table with a similar case, which Jack regarded suspiciously.

'High denomination,' said Carlson, nodding to the thug, who opened the case.

It contained ten slim bundles of five-thousand Ecu notes. Jack counted the notes, checking the circuitry imprinted in the paper of each with the anti-forge scanner set in his watch. Carlson checked each and every one of the cubes with his personal unit. When they had finished they sat back, Carlson watching him carefully and Jack studying Carlson's dubious companions.

'I do hope there are going to be no further ... dealings,' Jack suggested.

Carlson stretched his back, fiddled with his nose ring and smiled weakly. 'Of course not. As you said, "a good price". Tell me ... these new implants from Osaka...'

Jack smiled as that something squirmed impatiently within him. 'They are very effective.' He picked up an aluminium ash tray, crumpled it like paper into a ball in one hand then dropped it on the table top. Carlson stared at it expressionlessly as Gene sneezed and shivered and the thugs warily shifted in their seats.

Jack took up the case of money and headed for the door. The Chinaman stood aside for him and he was soon on the street and walking quickly away.

Done, finished.

The attack came two streets away. Suddenly his left arm felt very light, strange. He lifted it and, without understanding, stared at the smoking stump of his wrist. Smoke burst from his jeans at his hip, then from his shirt.

Laser.

Suddenly he was running, faster than he had ever run before. A woman screamed next to him, but by the time she began falling he was ten yards beyond her and accelerating. A store front window flickered red and the manikin inside caught flame and slumped like a man without bones, but by then Jack had darted into the alleyways and was gone.

Jack collapsed behind the rubbish skip, his body awash with pain and the case of money clutched in his right hand as if welded there.

Bastards ... a laser ... the bleeding.

He looked around vaguely for something to use as a tourniquet, then peered down at the stump of his left wrist and saw that it was as dry as biltong.

Am I dying?

But no, the pain was fading and his head clear. He sat upright and wondered what he must do now.

They cut my fucking hand off.

He had to recover his hand. He had the money, and there were freelance surgeons enough in Sao Paulo, just like the ones who came here to offer expensive cosmetic surgery to the likes of Carlson. Jack forced himself to his feet, searched the skip and found some black plastic, which he awkwardly wrapped around his butchered wrist.

Why do I feel so calm?

But he knew that was a question he need not ask. He felt calm because he had been made to feel calm, just as his fear and anger had been controlled, his strength, his speed, his bleeding. Something that had lain dormant in cometary ice for God knows how many millennia, now resided in his body, and perhaps in the bodies of others...

On the streets again Jack bought a long coat to cover his blood-stained clothing, not that it was noticeable in the neon and hololight. He bought food, lots of food, and bottles of glucose tablets. Then he bought a small portable cooler to hang on his belt, stowed his money in a street safe, and headed back towards the Cicero.

He found his hand in the gutter where it had been kicked, lying like some fat cave-dwelling spider. As the crowds passed him without a glance, he scooped it up and dropped it into the cooler. As he stood up he saw a long black hydrogen-powered sedan pull up outside the Cicero, and Carlson, Gene, and his four men climbing into it. Carlson was agitated: waving his arms about and shouting to one of his men. Jack felt an anger that brought him round with sickening lurch.

Not now. No, not now.

He fought against what roiled inside him, tried to damp his anger, and he turned away. There was a time limit. This he knew. If he was to save his hand he had to get to a surgeon as quickly as possible. Carlson could wait to die. Jack walked away.

The sign said 'Doctor Benedict Jones' whilst underneath were listed all the services catered for, including plastic surgery, augmentation, and much else besides. Jack pushed open the panelled door and walked in, scanning the waiting room.

Everything was clinically white; comfortable seats were scattered around low glass coffee tables on a tough cream carpet. A young man in a business suit sat in one of the chairs reading a portable console, the side of his head shaven and a dressing over what Jack supposed to be the connections for a cerebral augmentation. From behind a desk of painfully white plastic, a nurse with rainbow-dyed hair and a blue uniform glanced up from her nails and squinted at him suspiciously. Jack was in a hurry. He strode to her desk and took out a wad a five-thousand Ecu notes.

'I need attention right now,' he said.

She stared at the money as she dropped her cosmetics in her handbag. 'What ... do you require,' she asked, then added, 'sir.'

Jack could think of no other way to put it. He held up the stump of his wrist. 'My hand has been severed.' He opened the cold box at his side and showed her its contents. She paled and sat back.

'One moment.' She got up and hurried to the side door of the waiting room.

Jack turned away from the desk, glanced at the business-suited man, then took a seat. He was at a loss to know what else to do. He felt no pain, and as a consequence he felt much like a man who had come in to have repairs made on his car.

Jones came into the waiting room after a couple of minutes, studied Jack for a second then gestured him to follow. The receptionist came out to her desk and sat down again.

Jones led him down a corridor, past a room where a woman lay on a table with a loom of wires plugged into her head. He took him into another room much the same and instructed him to lie on the table.

'What medication have you taken?'

'None,' said Jack, and this evinced surprise.

'I have to know else there could be mistakes with the anaesthesia.'

'As I said, I have taken nothing. This has only just happened.'

Jones stared at him for a moment then said, 'Right, I'll put you out now, that way there will be little pain. That'll be five thousand dollars down.'

Jack reached into his pocket and pulled out a five thousand Ecu note, which was near twice the amount. Jones took the note and pocketed it then he reached down and unhooked the cold-box from Jack's belt.

'Laser,' he said as he dropped Jack's hand into tin tray. Then he took up a multi syringe and primed it. Jack felt a terrible urge to avoid the syringe and run, but he suppressed the urge long enough for a sheet of blackness to cover him.

Chapter Three

Out of the blackness, like a potholer coming up after a week's subterranean journeying. Lights were bright all around him and the smell of disinfectant astringent in his nostrils. A surge of adrenaline jerked him upright even as the nurse pulled the mask from his face. Jones and the nurse gaped at him in shock.

'That is the quickest recovery I have ever seen,' said Jones.

Jack studied at his re-attached hand, now splinted and bound.

'How did it go?'

'There was some dead tissue, and unfortunately some of the nerves could not be reconnected since they were too severely damaged.'

Jack slid his legs off of the table and jerked a drip from his arm. The nurse moved to protest, but Jones caught her arm and held her back.

'What is it?' Jones asked, 'Some sort of augmentation? Drugs? A PCP derivative? Nobody recovers this quickly.'

'How much more do I owe you?' asked Jack.

Jones looked askance at the nurse before picking up a pad from a table scattered with instruments. 'One moment.'

'Just give me an estimate.'

'This is not so—'

'An estimate.'

'You'll probably be in credit. It will be in the region of four thousand Ecu.'

Jack liked him for that, for he could have demanded more.

'Keep the change,' he said, and headed for the door.

Two constables sat in the waiting room, in chairs by the wall, drinking coffee. Jack glanced at them and continued on through. The door opened behind him, and he saw one of the constables glance aside, then leap to his feet, spilling his coffee in the process. Just like Jones they had not expected him to recover so quickly.

Slow motion.

Jack whipped round and stepped towards them, back-handed the one who had risen. The man hit the wall and slid down senseless. His companion tried to rise but Jack brought his hand back in a flat slap that laid the man out on the floor. Then he paused and studied what he had wrought. He was proud of himself, for he had not killed them. He moved to go, but changed his mind when he saw the weaponry one of them was carrying. Both of them carried stun batons, but the one he had struck first must have been a 'special' for at his hip, in a security holster, he wore a twenty-millimetre flack gun. Jack reached down, broke the armoured holster open as if it was made of brittle toffee then, tucking the gun under his jacket, exited the surgery. Jones and the nurse were long gone, perhaps hiding in their aseptic operating theatres.

Carlson was scared. Gene knew this because he was no longer trying to fondle her in his usual contemptuous manner; no longer displaying his power and control to his juniors, his virtual ownership of her – or perhaps the dose of flu she seemed to have picked up was putting him off. He sat in the car as tense as a wire, his hand wandering to the comfort of the Tosh holstered under his jacket. All four of his men, including the driver, were likewise armed for this trip to the Cicero, which had become almost obligatory to Carlson since Jack Smith's escape. Carlson dared not show his fear in any obvious manner.

'He's probably long gone by now, or dead in some alley,' said Gene, by way of desultory comfort. She was bored and fed up now and felt like hell. Her payment from Carlson had not been quite enough for her to make a break from him and she was coming to regret some of her choices. Jack, if he had survived, was carrying near a hundred-thousand Ecus. Perhaps she could have made the break with him? It wouldn't have been so bad. Some of his habits were a bit disgusting, but at least they did not cause her the pain of some of Carlson's little games. Carlson glanced at her with annoyance then gazed out the window as they pulled up outside the Cicero.

'That may be the case—' he began, and got no further.

The explosion frosted the screen and it seemed as if the driver was turning to say something, yet the side of his face was gone. Gene screamed as Carlson groped for his Tosh. A second explosion jerked one of the front seats back and the driver's companion spurted his life out through burst upholstery over Gene's legs. She screamed some more.

'Out!' yelled Carlson, and the two remaining heavies exited their doors with a well-rehearsed roll, their Toshes coming from their holsters with practised ease.

'Shit! What's he got! Shut up!'

Gene shut up, thinking with some calm part of her mind that Jack must have got hold of either police- or military-issue weaponry. She sneezed and dropped down to the floor. Irrelevantly she realized she was ravenously hungry, and even the raw eggs Jack enjoyed seemed appetizing now. Carlson was swearing unremittingly as he crouched down beside her.

Through the doors Gene could hear the static hissing of the Toshes, then she heard another sound: the familiar whoosh of a police-issue twenty. The explosion threw slivers of glass into her hair. The car jerked and she saw one of its doors bowling down the street. People were screaming and running out there, and Gene moved to where the door had been torn away, ready to run too. She saw one of Carlson's men stand, fire, then be blown to bloody fragments, his head hitting the sidewalk still attached to a length of spine. She rolled out of the car. It was a death trap, and to hell with Carlson. A glance over the car showed her something moving so fast it was hard to identify. A man? The figure blurred past the second of Carlson's men, who he fell slowly to the road with the top of his head missing. Gene sat down on the pavement in plain view.

Jack. She had no weapons against him, not when he was like that, God, not like that.

'I made you a promise, Carlson.'

The voice seemed disembodied, seemed to come out of the very air.

'We can talk about this! We can work something out!'

Carlson was edging towards Gene's side of the car. She saw that he had a shock grenade in his hand. Gene stood up. She could not fight; she had no weapons that killed. With a flick of her hand she undid a few of the buttons on her waistcoat. Then she saw him: thin as a scarecrow, nail-head eyes remorseless in a death's head, a twenty clutched in his left hand.

'I don't want to die,' she said, wondering if her words would have any effect.

'You don't have to.'

The shock grenade went off with a candent red flash, but even as the blast threw her back Gene knew that it had missed Jack, or rather, that he had avoided it. Then an arm snaked round her neck and a Tosh wedged under her chin.

'I don't know what you value, Jack Smith, but if you value her then you come out and drop that twenty.' Carlson's voice was harsh in Gene's ear. She could feel him shaking.

Jack walked out from behind a Ford up on bricks and scarred with smoking Tosh burns. He sauntered out with the twenty slack at his side.

'I value her a little,' he said, his words clipped and his voice strained. 'I have it under control at the moment.' He paused for a second and, when there was no reply, went on as if what he was saying should be obvious to them. 'It's the anger at the moment, but it knows that she ... she is the same.' He dropped the twenty on the ground.

Carlson's Tosh came up, levelled, fired. Gene saw a shop front erupt twenty feet back from where Jack had been standing, before as she flung Carlson's arm away. As she hit the ground Jack was there, Carlson's wrist gripped in his right hand. She heard the sickening crunch of bone and Carlson's girlish scream, then he slammed against the car and the scream truncated. And Jack was bending over her.

'Are you alright?'

Of course she was all right, but Carlson? She looked past Jack. The Tosh was in Carlson's left hand, Jack turning and moving. Gene held up her hand as if to halt time.

A bright and terrible pain took her away.

The street was empty of life, empty of movement, but for Jack. He picked up what remained of Carlson and tossed it across the bonnet of the car, an offering perhaps to the woman he could not save and had not precisely known why he had wanted to. Sirens howled close by and like a wraith he fled into the shadows.

Medical Examiner Estefan was tall and thin with hands that twitched and leapt like insects. His hair was grey and tied back in a pony tail that he trapped under his lab coat. As if the years of autopsies had given him contempt for human life and its foibles, his expression was acerbic. Jane noted he had an oddly-shaped silver ring in one ear and wondered if this designated his sexual preference. He had shown little interest in her thus far – a lack of reaction she was unused to – and was all business.

'Jane Ulreas? Did I pronounce that correctly?'

She nodded.

'Your fields are helminthology and entomology, specializing in arthropod parasites. Is that correct?'

'I prefer to simply call myself a parasitologist,' she said with irritation. She was tired and jet-lagged and in no mood for indulging in semantic discussions. She turned to Chris, marvelling anew at his changelessness. 'That would be about right, wouldn't it?'

Chris smiled benevolently and nodded. 'That is etymologically correct in a general sense.'

Jane turned away, envying Chris not only his changelessness but his perfect pronunciation of polysyllables.

'And you are..?' enquired Estefan, touching his fingers to his bottom lip and staring at Chris intently. Jane contained the disgust that had been inculcated into her as a member of that generation called the New Puritans, who grew to adulthood in Europe during the time of the AIDS III epidemic. She had seen the expression, now on Estefan's face, on the faces of so many when they gazed upon Chris's Apollonian perfection.

In that smoothly modulated voice Chris said, 'I am Chris Golem. I am Professor Ulreas's assistant.'

'Hmm,' said Estefan, his hand sliding down to his chin. Then, remembering himself, he led the way into the mortuary.

As the doors swung shut behind them, Jane could smell strong disinfectant overlaying a hint of corruption.

'I think only one branch of your knowledge may be required ... the helminthology,' said Estefan.

'Worms,' said Jane as they came to the sheeted figure under the panel lights. She noted the fluids spattered on the sheet then peered to the lab technician who was cleaning instruments at a bench along the far wall.

'Get Miss Ulreas and Mr Golem a coat each, Smythe.'

Smythe glanced round, paused, then turned round for a better look. 'Why certainly,' he said.

That's more like it, thought Jane, then felt ashamed of her vanity.

'Here,' Estefan handed her a tube with 'Anosmic Gel' printed on it in ice-blue letters. She accepted it and, to show that she knew precisely what it was for, squeezed some out and wiped it under her nose. It immediately numbed her sense of smell – a lack she always associated with open bodies.

'Mr Golem?'

Jane watched as Chris took the tube and wiped some of its contents round his nostrils. It seemed for a moment as if his expression was one of resigned annoyance, but that, of course, was impossible. Estefan took the tube back, touching Chris's fingers unnecessarily, Jane thought, then dropped it into his top pocket and turned to the corpse. Smythe next brought their coats, and they both put them on as Estefan pulled back the sheet with a dramatic flourish. Jane repressed the urge to turn away. The bodies she was mostly used to dealing with were of animals. Here lay a young woman opened out like a fish, her ribs splayed out like fingers and most of her internal organs removed. Jane stepped forwards, Chris just behind her, peering over her shoulder.

'Helminthology, you said.'

Wordlessly Estefan pointed to the bottom of the cavity left by the removal of the woman's intestines and liver. Clinging along her spine was a white, segmented worm. It could, perhaps, have been mistaken for part of her spine, so closely was it intertwined with her vertebrae, had it not moved. Jane was fascinated, her repulsion forgotten.

'Probe,' she said, holding out her hand to the lab technician as if she were back in her laboratory in Cornwall rather than half a world away. In a moment he placed a Perspex light-wand in her hand. Jane poked at the worm.

'Long, segmented like a cestode ... has to be some sort of cestode ... you don't get trematodes of this size ...'

'Cestode?' said Smythe.

'Tapeworm,' said Estefan.

Jane glanced up at him. He would not be easy to fool. In his work he must have encountered numerous parasites, since this part of the world was swarming with them.

'No scolex ... head ...' Jane pushed aside one of the segments and noted a thin bundle of fibres like ganglia penetrating between the host's vertebrae. She explored further and found the same fibres spreading across rib bones, some severed and hanging loose.

'What did these fibres penetrate?'

Estefan sounded embarrassed. 'The heart, lungs, liver ... all the major organs and glands. We didn't notice—'

Jane interrupted, 'This killed her?'

'No,' said Estefan, and seemed to relish pulling the sheet back further to expose the woman's head, or rather what remained of it. Her lower jaw and part of her neck had been burnt away. 'Some sort of gang warfare in the lower city. She was hit by a Tosh.'

'A Tosh?' said Jane.

It was Chris who answered, 'A form of particle burst hand gun manufactured by the Toshiba Corporation in Japan.'

Jane stared at him long and hard, wondering where he had got that little piece of information, then turned back to Estefan. 'Have there been others like this?' She did not refer to the manner of the woman's death, as she knew it likely to be quite common in Sao Paulo.

'No, this is the first, but an order has been issued to everyone with med-scan licences to report anything like—'

'Do you have formalin, glycerine, Zenkers fluid etcetera?'

Estefan seemed taken aback. 'Of course.'

Keep him off-balance.

'Canada balsam, hydroplastic?'

'Yes...'

Jane peered at the parasite again.

'You were lucky I was here at the conference,' she said, hoping that Chris would keep his mouth shut. 'Would it be possible for me to investigate a little further?'

'That is dependent on the coroner, relatives ...' but Estefan was staring at Chris hungrily and Jane knew she would get her chance.

'I would very much like to investigate further.'

Estefan glanced at her. 'Do you know what it is?'

Jane smiled and nodded.

Not a word Chris. Not a word.

She said, 'It's one of the taenia solium or a new form of Echinococcus cestoda, which of course would be quite interesting. We don't get much of a chance to see specimens like this in England and of course this branch of helminthology is one of my main interests.'

Don't lay it on too thick.

She held out her hands and smiled. 'In the interests of international co-operation?' It was a standing joke in most scientific communities since the war fought in Antarctica, a joke Estefan appreciated.

'I am sure something can be arranged.'

Later, as Jane and Chris walked through the park grounds of the hospital to their waiting police transport. Chris said, 'Taenia solium or a new form of Echinococcus cestoda?'

Jane would have thought him guilty of sarcasm, but that was impossible, quite impossible.

'Bullshit baffles brains,' she said. 'I've never seen nor heard of a parasite like that one before now.'

When Jack left the Rio Hotel, Gene would not have recognized him, but then, the condition Gene was in at that moment, he would not have recognized her. He was clean, for the first time in months, wore new jeans, a sweatshirt, jacket, and trainers, all comfortably fitting his shrunken frame. His face was cleanly shaven and his blond hair cropped close to his skull. He felt good as well: no cold-like symptoms, no bleeding, and in the past couple of weeks he had put on weight. Only the movement of that something deep inside him served to remind him that perhaps things were not well.

At the pavement he flagged a hydrocab, climbed in and seated himself comfortably. The driver, a shabby Puerto Rican, tapped the touch plate on his meter and looked round with a raised eyebrow.

'Nearest big pharmacy with med-scan facilities,' said Jack, surprised at this driver's reticence. The driver nodded and entered the chaotic flow of traffic with a suicidal lunge. And his reticence soon transformed into a flow of swearing that made even Jack's ears burn.

The pharmacy had half a street of glass frontage and at least ten street doors. Jack paid off the driver, fought his way across the pavement and through one door, and then waded into crowds impossibly more dense than those on the streets. Inside, the place was like a cavernous shopping centre. He soon saw a sign advertising med-scan facilities and forced his way towards it. Again something inside him was enjoying being surrounded by a mass of people and he wondered if that was truly part of him. He knew there was something poised inside him, ready to evoke fear or anger, and he intended to find out what it was. Suddenly the crowds parted and he found himself at the edge of a space occupied by three constables. Two of them crouched, pinning a woman to the ground, the third lying on his side clutching at his mouth, a pool of blood before his face in which a couple of teeth lay glistening.

'Bitch!' shouted one of the constables, and cracked the woman across the back of her head with a stun baton. Her struggles subsided somewhat, but she should have been unconscious. Jack faded back and observed from behind a dumpy black woman loaded down with carrier bags full of shopping which must have weighed half as much as she did. Soon all three of the constables were on their feet, the injured one staggering like a drunkard. They dragged the woman through a channel that automatically opened up through the crowds for them. Jack caught snippets of conversation.

'Christos! She moved like a snake!'

'... every damn one fights or runs ...'

'Bastard PVs!'

Jack moved over to the small balding man who, by his white coat with his name badge on it, obviously ran the med-scan facility.

'What was all that about?'

The man looked at him lugubriously and shook his head. 'Another PV, that's the third I've had today. Anyone would think them guilty of some crime the way they react, but they're only being taken to Central Hospital.' He turned away and surveyed the crowd as if wondering where all the madness was coming from.

'PVs?' asked Jack.

'Oh,' said the man glancing back at him, 'parasite victims. Some sort of parasite going around. The first was detected about two weeks ago, in the corpse of some woman killed in the lower city. All med-scan facilities have been told to report...' His gaze wondered away.

Parasite.

It shifted inside him and he knew.

Jesus! Something living inside me!

He remembered a premillennial flat-screen science fiction film adapted for holovision and subsequently voted least favourite film of the year by those on the TCC station. A creature had gestated inside a man then chewed its way out in bloody Caesarean. Jack rubbed his hand across his chest and broke out in a cold sweat. Inside him that something writhed.

'What does it do? This parasite?'

'Oh,' said the man, gazing at Jack as if wondering why he was still there. 'Not much known at present, though I imagine there are the usual symptoms of worm infestation; allergic reactions, bleeding, cirrhosis, lung disease...' He trailed off, swinging his attention back to the crowds again.

That confirms it, thought Jack.

'How is it spread?'

The man shrugged, then abruptly turned and studied Jack contemplatively. 'Are you here for a scan?'

Jack shook his head. 'No, just passing.' He moved away.

Back on the street again Jack now noticed a heavier than usual police presence and even a couple an army tank parked at a nearby junction.

As he remembered something fibrous locked in ice, he wondered if he was now seeing the first results of his crime. He stopped at the kerb and glanced up in time to see an armoured car trundle past. Suddenly he saw, with an unaccustomed clarity, what was to come. He had to get out of Sao Paulo, out of Brazil, and if possible, out of South America. The urge to run at that moment was difficult to suppress.

Chris forgot nothing, and he was incapable of making mistakes, so it was a comfort for Jane that he did not dispute her conclusions from the last week of research.

'It's doing something on a molecular level, those fibres fray down to less than a micron in diameter and seem to spread through the system, penetrating every cell in their path. It's doing something to the nervous system and the immune system. It has its fingers in every pie. Its physical structure is like a ganglion. We can find no cellular structure, no DNA. We don't know how it reproduces. As yet there is no sign of eggs of any kind. We haven't a clue to its vector, life cycle, whether it is infective at this stage. Have I missed anything?'

'The equipment is inadequate here,' said Chris smoothly.

Jane slumped into an armchair, reached for her bottle of aquavit and poured out two very thick fingers.

'Go on,' she said, then drank thirstily.

'What is required is a good scatology laboratory for the search for eggs or what may be the equivalent of some kind of miracidium if that is the way the parasite's young escape the host. That is perhaps irrelevant at this point as we as yet have no idea as to how it functions. For the study of what we assume to be the adult parasite, a modern cellular biology research facility is required. Here, all they have is a faulty scanning tunnelling electron microscope, and a primitive X-ray diffractor.'

Jane put her glass down. 'Well put, but the parasite is here, for now. How many cases so far?'

Chris said, 'Five hundred and seventy-three. Of those only a hundred and twenty are in confinement at Central Hospital. Two hundred went for relocation. The rest are dead.'

'Bloody police, and military. It's no wonder they run or fight.'

'It is strange that not one host has been taken without pursuit or violence. Also, fifty- two of the three hundred and seventy-three died in the hospital, some attempting to escape, some suiciding once discovering what was inside them.'

Jane stared at the wall remembering the screams of a man bound in a straitjacket:

'It's taking me over! It's taking me over!'

Somehow that man had ripped out of his jacket and thrown himself through a toughened glass window on the seventh floor.

'What the hell are we dealing with here, Chris?'

'A creature like nothing before on Earth.'

There, it was said. Jane had not wanted to say it or even think it:

Like nothing on Earth.

The ETO – extra-terrestrial organism – idea had been discussed a great deal in scientific circles, but never seriously.

Jane wondered what her colleagues would think now if she told them there was an organism on Earth not based on nucleic acids and without a cellular structure. She had a horrible feeling they would laugh at her. At first. She shivered and gulped more aquavit, then she glanced up at Chris. 'Sit down, you make me nervous.'

Without comment Chris obliged, though it seemed to Jane that there was an expression almost of disapproval on his face. Not possible. She was anthropomorphising again.

'Rather than bemoaning our inadequacies and what we don't know, let's look more closely at what we do know: at the behavioural aspects. It shouldn't take long.'

Chris watched her with mild interest, it seemed.

'Those infected with the parasite show an inclination to be amongst crowds. This is probably something to do with how it is transmitted but doesn't necessarily mean the host is at the infective stage. New hosts, after an initial immunological reaction, have their systems boosted; they are faster and stronger, their fight and flight reactions are stronger. This then is the parasite acting upon its host to increase its own survivability – a not uncommon occurrence. There's that snail parasite that causes the snail to grow a thicker shell…'

A hammering at the door to their hotel room cut Jane off in mid stride.

'Who is it?'

'You are needed at Central Hospital, Miss Ulreas.'

Jane nodded to Chris, who stood and moved smoothly to the door. He opened it to a woman dressed in army fatigues, carrying a machine gun slung under her arm. She peremptorily pushed her way in.

'I am Major Branson, you are to accompany me to the Hospital, Miss Ulreas. General Stark wishes a report on your work.'

'And who the hell is General Stark?' asked Jane, glancing nervously at the two soldiers standing outside the door.

'General Stark is now in charge of the PV situation. As of ten o'clock this evening martial law was declared. This is a serious problem.'

Jane felt a horrible sinking feeling in the pit of her stomach.

Serious problem. Not half as serious as it was about to become, she thought, as she stood up and downed the last of her aquavit.

'I'll come, but I don't know how I can help the General.'

Branson said nothing, but the look she flicked over Jane showed her contempt. *Dyke*, thought Jane, as she followed her out, then wished she could control such New Puritan reactions. It was a comfort to have Chris at her side, and certainly the New Puritans would never have approved of him.

They were taken to a personnel carrier with metal seats not designed for comfort. Jane noted how empty the streets were as they drove to hospital. Things had been getting ugly for some time, ever since the parasite victims had been dehumanised into PVs, yet she had stayed, against the advice of the embassy. The PV situation, as it seemed the military mind had come to call it, appeared to be the best of excuses to start killing people, just as the 'AIDS VII situation' in central Africa had been fifteen years back. She glanced at Chris and wondered what he thought; how his clear and painfully sharp mind perceived this situation.

The personnel carrier passed through a newly erected barrier around the hospital and into the grounds, which now swarmed with troops like worshippers round armoured cars like altars. Directly in front of the hospital there now stood a row of sinister-looking matt green trucks. Major Branson led them inside then to the hospital director's office, now being used as an operations room. General Stark looked up as they entered, acknowledged the Major's salute, then studied Jane and Chris with the same contempt Jane had seen in the Major's face. *Oh God, another rigor mortis brain,* she thought as she nodded and smiled. The General stood.

'Please, have a seat Miss Ulreas. You too, Mr Golem.'

Jane noted how the seats were well back from the desk and set well apart. *Better to isolate you Grandma.* Jane picked up her seat and moved it closer to the desk. Chris did likewise with his. The General seemed for a moment as if he was going to order them shot, then he grudgingly sat down.

'Now, Miss Ulreas, this PV situation is really getting out of hand. Do you have a cure as yet?'

Jane nearly burst out laughing. Military mind: it seemed a contradiction in terms.

'There seems to be, as yet, no way of killing or flushing this parasite. We've tried all the usual drugs and even some of the old ones like the chloroethylenes. Surgery is out of the question as by the time the parasite is detected it's too closely linked to the host to be removed.'

'Is it sexually transmitted?'

'Now there's a question. We have seen no signs that it might be, though as yet we do not know how it is transmitted. This is always a complex problem with parasites. We cannot even be sure if what we have found is its infective stage.'

She noticed how his eyes had seemed to glaze over when she said, 'complex problem'. She knew that the military mind did not like complex problems.

She said, 'I think the only way forward now is for me take samples back to England for study. The facilities here are not ... quite what is required.'

He seemed not to have heard her. 'How best, would you suggest, might this parasite be exterminated.'

Jane did not like that word and at that moment she remembered another word she had heard only recently: 'relocation'. Two hundred parasite victims had been relocated. They had been relocated by the military. A trickle of sweat ran down her backbone as she thought about the trucks outside.

'I do not think there is as yet any way to ... exterminate this parasite.'

Stark stared at her for a long moment then turned to Chris. 'Have you anything to add Mr Golem?'

'I have nothing to add,' said Chris mildly.

Stark glanced towards Major Branson and nodded his head.

Jane said, 'I haven't got enough—' A hand grasped her round the upper arm and jerked her out of her seat. 'What is this?' She saw a soldier try to jerk Chris up out of his seat, fail to do so, then step back and draw his pistol. Chris stood and walked ahead of him to the door whilst Jane was hustled along after. She knew what this was now, all too clearly she saw the coming pattern of events. The 'PV situation' was the excuse to initiate a military take over, and the military might not want any inconvenient, expert, observers. The official at the embassy had warned her:

'The situation is delicate here at the moment. I would suggest to you that when the biochemistry conference ends you leave Brazil at once.'

Why hadn't she listened?

They were taken along a corridor to a lift, then down to another corridor that led to a dark room, cleared of beds and other inconvenient medical trivialities. Jane stared at the bullet holes in the walls. Chris is a comfort, she thought, but that is all. He was as incapable of action as a calculator. A gun clicked.

Oh shit!

Jane closed her eyes. There were two dull thuds then the shatteringly loud explosion of automatic fire. She was still alive. She opened her eyes to a scene she could hardly comprehend at first. The two soldiers lay on the floor, unconscious or dead. Major Branson was backed up against a wall, her face pale, terror etching her features. Chris stood before her holding her machine gun. Jane saw that he had been hit with the full clip; synthetic skin had been flayed from his chest by the bullets to expose gleaming ceramal underneath. None of them had known. None of them had known what Chris was. He dropped the machine gun, and then tapped the Major on the side of her head with perhaps one tenth of his strength. She slumped bonelessly to the floor.

'You're not supposed to harm anyone,' Jane blurted. Their captors were only unconscious, but androids were just not supposed to hurt human beings. There were laws weren't there?

Chris turned to her with what could not be mistaken for anything other than a smile of satisfaction. 'Whatever gave you that curious idea,' he said.

Peter Mendelssohn was scared, but that was nothing unusual; he had been scared for more than a year now, ever since he found out what his employer was really like. He controlled his fear and just got on with his job though. Today he would complete work on this little beauty then it would be back to his own project. He stood with his grip shoes holding the industrial carpet in his null gee lab and his bony hands in the pockets of his lab coat. With piercing blue eyes he studied the weapon, now held into a clamp and linked into all the test gear.

'You cannot fire an anti-photon weapon in this laboratory,' said Lilly, the station AI.

'Obviously,' he replied, 'but this test will show if it's working properly. What does Haven want it for?'

There was no reply. He had expected none. His access to Lilly was limited, but substantially more than the Toad would have wanted. With his shoes making a scrunching sound on the carpet he walked over to a keyboard and quickly rattled over a few keys.

PARAMETERS: SET ERSATZ BURST TO COMPLETE MOLECULAR DISRUPTION OF A HUMAN BEING.

He should have known. He keyed in the instruction for the test then walked over to his bench, sat down, and continued to assemble something silvery and beautiful. One day soon he knew he would be summoned to a personal meeting with his boss. He had no intention of going.

Chapter Four

Armed police were everywhere, but none of them bothered Jack. It was surprising how a suit and a briefcase lent an air of respectability, and the mirrored sunglasses an air of menace. He had deliberately cultivated the look of a member of the secret police, who were never that secret. The woman at the HOTOL desk gazed at him warily and checked his passport before giving him his boarding card.

'Gate seven at ten fifty. It will come up on the screens.'

He nodded and smiled a polite thank-you and headed for the cafeteria. He had twenty minutes to wait. At the cafeteria he got himself a cup of coffee and sat down, removing his sunglasses as he did so. Then he looked around.

There was a hint of hysteria in the air. The people here had an anxiety to be gone from this place sharper than that of homesick tourists. In a matter of days Sao Paulo had turned from a bustling centre of commerce to a city under siege. The streets were mostly empty, but for the armoured cars and squads of soldiers patrolling the pavements. A large percentage of the population was staying indoors, waiting, expectant. Jack thought that they might not have much longer to wait. Already there had been shootings after curfew and tell-tale stains on the pavements in the morning. With an air of casualness he opened his briefcase and took out a portable console. Across the other side of the airport foyer he saw that soldiers were checking people's passports. He also noted the abruptly nervous air of the blond woman sitting only a table away from him.

His passport was fine, Jack knew this, he was a British subject, but he wondered if his description had been circulated.

There had been the encounter at the surgeon's and that bloody encounter in the lower city. What could he do? The parasite shifted uneasily inside him. Run or fight. Run or fight. He tried to ignore it, but was finally driven to his feet. The soldiers, three of them, were heading in his direction. He glanced at them, picked up his briefcase, and headed at a forced leisurely pace for the toilets. He perfectly distinguished the sound of their footsteps from the riotous noise in the airport foyer, just as he had been able to with the killers Carlson had sent after him. They turned to follow him. In a moment he entered the toilets and moved to a sink to wash his hands. The door banged open and the three soldiers crowded through.

'Passport,' snapped one of them at Jack's shoulder.

'One moment please,' said Jack and moved to dry his hands. Just then a man came out of one of the toilet booths, doing up his shirt as if perhaps he had just changed. Jack was struck by his almost flawless features. He looked like a Greek god. The man moved to pass the soldiers, but one of them turned on him.

'You, wait!'

Jack continued to dry his hands.

'I said passport!' snapped the soldier at Jack's shoulder and caught hold of his upper arm.

Nooo...

It was too late. He reacted. He backhanded the soldier and sent him crashing into a condom machine. The second one began to raise his weapon. Jack shoved the weapon aside, drove a fist into his stomach instantly followed by an elbow to the temple, dropping him. However, his next move stalled. The other soldier was down. The blond god studied Jack with a mild curiosity.

'You move very fast,' he said.

'You're no slouch yourself,' said Jack. 'I take it you don't want the military paying too much attention to you?'

'You likewise?'

Jack nodded and hauled one of the soldiers up by his belt and carried him to one of the toilet booths.

'You are also very strong. May I know your name?'

'Jack Smith.'

'My name is Chris Golem.'

Jack paused while seating the soldier on the toilet. 'Would that be the Chris Golem who was working at Central Hospital with Professor Ulreas?'

'The same.'

Jack found plastic ties at the soldier's belt and bound him in position. He then ripped the soldier's shirt and gagged him with it. Leaning out of the booth he said, 'I could do with some help here,' and then fell silent. Chris held a soldier in each hand, up off the floor by their belts, their arms and legs trailing on the floor, and as casually as if he was carrying dustbin bags he hoisted each of them into a booth.

The parasite? Possibly, yet he did not think so.

'Are you augmented, Chris?' he asked.

'After a fashion,' said Chris as he bound and gagged the two soldiers.

They locked the doors to the booths, then climbed out again. Together they left the toilet, just as a man with a young boy entered. Chris smiled at them benevolently. Jack put on his sun glasses.

The blond woman was searching through her handbag as they came to the cafeteria, a constable standing next to her. Jack made to turn away, then hesitated as Chris continued on. Professor Ulreas? It seemed strange to him that this voluptuous woman was a professor. She was a parasitologist, he knew this.

Viewing the situation ahead of him he felt the urge to run, but it was not as strong as his urge to learn things about himself. He followed Chris and, by the time they reached the table, the constable was studying Jane's passport.

'Is there any problem, officer?' asked Chris.

The constable looked up. 'Are you Chris Golem?'

Chris smiled, then his hand snapped out so fast that Jack hardly saw it, and rapped the constable on his temple. The man slumped but the hand come down and caught hold of his collar and held him upright.

'Now what?' said Jack.

Chris glanced around again then caught the constable's belt and guided him to a seat. It was a feat of strength Jack doubted he could perform. It seemed as if the man had quite naturally taken a seat, with Chris's hand on his back in a friendly fashion. Jack peered down at Jane.

'Which flight are you taking?' he asked.

'The HOTOL to London,' she replied after a momentary hesitation.

'Now, might be a good time to try and board.'

'Yes,' she said, nodding vigorously.

Chris's hands were a blur by the constable, and they left him bound with plastic ties, leaning forwards over the table with his chin cupped in his hands.

At passport control waited two more police officers and a soldier carrying a formidable looking assault rifle. As he and his new companions approached, Jack felt sure that this was the end of the line for them. Then came the muffled sound of gun shots from the foyer. Jack glanced round but could not locate the source, but guessed one of the soldiers in the toilet must have regained consciousness and got to his gun. The soldier and the two constables rushed out into the foyer, and the HOTOL steward took their boarding cards and ushered them quickly through, obviously as eager to be gone as they were.

'Most fortuitous,' said Chris, and Jack envied his calm. Only when he was seated with his case on his lap and the HOTOL screaming down the runway did the tension drain out of him.

The HOTOL lifted into the stratosphere and was soon travelling at Mach ten. Jack had managed to get into one of the seats near Jane Ulreas, and was eager to initiate conversation.

'What was the trouble for you back there?' he asked, directing his question at Jane rather than her companion. He still did not know what to make of Chris. She studied him, then glanced at Chris as if seeking reassurance before replying.

'I was there studying the ...' her voice turned contemptuous, 'parasite situation.'

'Yes, I heard something about that,' said Jack. He glanced aside, but Chris still wore the same mildly interested expression.

Jane went on, 'The military decided to use it as an excuse to step in. They didn't want any witnesses to ... to what they intended to do.'

'And that was?'

'We believe they intended to kill all the PVs and institute an extermination program. Remember the AIDS VII thing in Central Africa?'

'And they wanted to kill you as well?' asked Jack, forcing disbelief into his voice.

'Well,' said Jane with a sneer, 'that's the way the military mind works.'

'But you escaped,' he glanced at Chris, 'and I can guess how.'

'What about you? Chris told me what you did.'

'Sordid,' said Jack. 'I too ran afoul of the authorities. Tell me, this parasite, what do you know about it?'

Jane did not seem as glad to discuss this subject as he had expected. 'Too little,' she began, but then went on in measured tones to tell Jack all she and Chris had learned or surmised, as if getting it all clear in her own mind.

'It doesn't sound like anything I know of, but then I know little about parasites. Do parasites cause these sorts of ... symptoms? Can they make people stronger, alter their behaviour?'

'Parasites get into every possible niche,' said Jane in her lecturer's voice. 'Multiceps, in its intermediate host, which is normally a sheep or some other ruminant, can lodge in the skull or spinal cord. In one side of the brain it causes the animal to pull its head right round and circle in that direction, and vice versa. I saw a horse once that had the worm in its head. The poor thing had its head down between its forelegs and kept walking into trees, then just standing still there. It didn't last long. But then that's the evolutionary vector of that parasite, considering that its next host is a carnivore.'

Jack nodded then said, 'But surely that kind of behaviour is caused by pretty simple damage – is not so purposeful?'

Jane held up her hand. 'Purpose doesn't come into it, only selection. But take the brain worm. It's transmitted from an ant to a sheep. It burrows into the ant's brain and alters its behaviour in such a way that during the cool periods of the day the ant will climb up to the top of a grass stalk, cling on, and wait to be eaten by a passing sheep. There's another that is passed from a certain type of snail to birds. It causes the snail to lay itself out like a dinner.'

Jack bowed his head. 'They never act in the best interests of their hosts.'

'That is what separates parasitism from symbiosis and mutualism. A parasite obtains nutriment to the detriment of its host. Symbiosis is interdependence.'

'Mutualism?'

'Somewhere between the other two. It's sometimes difficult to draw definite lines between them all.'

'Could it be that this one is not necessarily a parasite?'

Jane gazed out of the window for a moment before replying. 'At the moment it seems to be, since not very many of those infected have lived through it. Some of them died from the allergic reaction, nerve disorders, or self-destructed because of the psychological stress. I wonder if it's likely that any of the victims will survive either it or the military.' She paused reflectively for a moment. 'But really we're overstepping the mark by trying to give it any of those labels.'

Chris leant forward. 'It is an extra-terrestrial organism.'

Jane stared at him as if she could not believe what he had said. Jack leant back in his seat and studied Chris, but could make nothing from his expression.

'You're probably right,' he said, knowing that they were. *Should I tell them?* He wondered. But reinforced instinct kept him quiet. He did not want to become a subject for study.

As they moved down the exit ramp, Jane noted that they had lost their intense companion, but did not let it bother her. Her concern was mainly for the samples they had brought back and the reaction of Her Majesty's Customs, since the samples could be classed as dangerous biological materials. She considered lying, but thought that with Chris with her she would not get away with it. He did not belong to her. He had just been provided by World Health.

'Well at least the parasite hasn't reached here yet,' she said, breathing the monoxide free air.

'I think that perhaps it has,' said Chris.

'What do you mean?'

'Your samples of course.'

Jane studied him suspiciously. He's a machine, she thought, but I must not forget just how complex a machine he is.

'I must find out about your programming someday,' she said, taking out her passport.

Likewise, Chris removed his passport. It was easier that way, she had been told, and Chris would probably take exception to travelling with the luggage. *What is the difference anyway,* she wondered, and answered herself immediately*: I am a complex machine pre-programmed by my genes for their transmission. He is a complex machine programmed by us and by AIs. I can beat my programming, contraception is one example, but can he?* The question seemed to slink off in her mind like a wounded rat, hidden, but she knew it was still there.

Once outside the airport Jack smiled to himself with relief. There had been a bad moment there in customs, but there were no currency restrictions on the Ecu. What had made the customs officials suspicious was that his entire luggage was full of wads of them. He supposed they had thought him a drugs baron escaping from the situation in Brazil with his ill-gotten gains. They had searched him and found nothing, checked his passport and found it valid, and then reluctantly let him go.

With the low, bone vibrating hum of gas turbines an aircab wafted down to him. He climbed inside and the driver, a strikingly attractive brunette, peered round at him.

'Where would you like to be taken?' she asked.

He stared at her for a moment, taking in the contrast of this to his most recent taxi ride in Sao Paulo, then he told her, 'Take me towards Maldon Island.'

Once it had been a coastal town on the river Blackwater. Now it stood on a peninsular jutting out from sea defences, surrounded by the sea. It amused Jack to think how badly penny-pinching councillors had erred. Much relieved to finally realize that they were not about to be swamped by melting ice caps, plans for building up and repairing of the sea wall had been shelved. However, the steady sea level rise since the last Ice Age and the steady subsidence of the East Coast had caught them out. That was all twenty years in the past now. The councillors were gone, and his house stood in a prime position on the new ten million pounds a mile sea defences.

'Please put your safety harness on.'

Jack obliged, the driver pulled back on her joystick and with a whining roar of turbines the taxi surfed into the sky. For the first time in quite a while Jack felt near to contentment. As the taxi hummed along under flocks of white clouds he gazed down at the familiar landscape with its patchwork of fields, scars of scraped out roads, and garden-roofed factory complexes. He was home. He had been away for far too long.

Soon the quarter-of-a-mile-wide mound that kept the sea out came into sight. Beyond it Jack could see the top branches of trees reaching from the water like pleading fingers, and surf breaking on the roofs of houses. The cab turned to run parallel to the wall on the way towards Maldon and Jack realized with a pang how close to home he was. He leant forward.

'Do you see that slab-laying machine?' he asked.

The brunette turned her head and squinted at the seaward side of the wall where a monstrous yellow beetle of a machine crawled on caterpillar treads along the forty-five degree face of the wall.

'I see it.'

'Landward of that and about half a mile further on there's a row of beach houses, amongst the trees.'

'Got them.'

'Take me there please.'

The aircab turned into the reflected glare from the sea. The driver put on a pair of sunglasses and began to hum to herself. In a moment they were spiralling down to the houses.

'That house,' said Jack, pointing to a house with plastic bank seals across the windows and doors and a garden returned to wilderness. The aircab set down on the overgrown lawn.

'I'll only be a moment.' He handed her a hundred Ecu note. 'Wait here please.' She took the note as if he had handed her a dirty postcard, glanced at the credit-card reader, then frowned. Jack got out of the car.

The house needed paint and the garden needed a lot of work. Trudging through the long grass Jack had to step round his robot mower, rusting where it had failed. Five years without maintenance had probably been too much to expect of it, or perhaps the power had been turned off. He did not know. He walked around to the back of the house, leant against a tilted stone sun dial and gazed out past a row of nettle elms to the sea. He felt nostalgia like pain. Five years. He had certainly paid for his wealth. He returned to the cab, noting that the meter had been turned off. Cash job. Things were not so different from Sao Paulo.

'Into Maldon please. Near as you can to the Ecubank.'

The aircab rose into the sky blasting leaves about it.

Jane Ulreas glanced aside from the screen of the nanoscope to the second screen with its multicoloured computer generated image from the x-ray diffractor. She blinked once or twice as if unsure of what she was seeing, then sat back in her chair and observed with chagrin the way the buttons of her old lab coat pulled against her breasts and stomach. The days of her voluptuousness were ending she decided. She was now definitely running too fat.

'Protein, protein, protein.' She shook her head, rested her fingers below the touch console, then sneezed. That was all she needed; a cold on top of everything else.

'Anything solid?' Chris asked in his smoothly modulated voice.

Jane repressed a bitter laugh as she peered down at her lab coat. God, did she need to lose weight.

'There are signs of snipping but it's difficult to tell what's been snipped out,' she said. 'We saw no sign of cancers or serious mutation so I would say it's only selfish DNA that's been snipped – the freeloaders on the genome. Chromosome length has definitely been shortened.'

Chris sat down next to her. 'What about the alleles?'

'Again: difficult to tell.'

'One would have thought the parasite would not have been able to tell the difference. It is logical to suppose that to increase its survivability in the organism it would make no distinction between selfish DNA and the alleles.'

'Don't be so pompous. It's not like you. We are, as you say, dealing with an ETO. It's capable of extremely complex manipulation yet it's killing its hosts. We cannot make—' Jane halted in mid-sentence and leant forward. That word: *survivability*. How could she have been so blind?

Fatals, my god! The fatals!

Her fingers blurred across the touch console and diffraction images flashed onto the screen next to Chris one after another, colours kaleidoscoping across his face.

'You have seen something,' he said.

Jane sat back again. 'The parasite can be called a protein engineer. Altered proteins are the cause of that killing allergic reaction. Now we know that it uses protein spliced RNA to alter the genome – to snip DNA – which in turn alters the RNA by transcription and the proteins that manufactures by translation. It's got its fingers in every pie to alter the entire vector of its host and increase its own survivability, or rather to *try* to increase its own survivability. That is if we forget about the dead for a moment,' which she could not do. 'What would you say would be the optimum thing for it to do to its host's DNA?'

There was a pause while Chris considered this. Jane had never known him to delay so long and because of this she knew that he had known before entering the room and had been edging her towards this.

'Optimum alteration would be for it to delete the fatals, or potential fatals; increasing its host's survivability would increase its own.'

'Right,' said Jane, trying to conceal her irritation, 'now scan this sample for known fatals.'

Chris reached for the console and the diffraction images became a flickering blur. Jane went on.

'Check them all: MS, susceptibility to known cancers – you know.'

The screen flickered to a standstill.

'I can find none.'

'Crafty little parasite,' said Jane. 'I bet its RNA templates cut down on copying errors as well.' She peered at the name at the corner of the screen. 'Poor bastard. If it hadn't killed him it might have made him live forever.'

'You suggest that it is trying to make its host ageless? What about its procreative process?'

Jane him suspiciously. He sounded pompous again.

'You tell me,' she said.

'If what you say is true then its procreative process must be through the human meiosis.'

'That's all we need; for this to be sexually transmitted. It'll make AIDS VII look like the common cold.' She sneezed. 'There have been no signs of it being passed on that way though. How about the faeces? Did scatology find anything in those samples we sent to them?'

'Fluke eggs and encysted cercariae. There are some unidentified samples but they suspect them to be pollen grains.'

'So we still don't know its vector.'

'Perhaps we are looking in the wrong place.'

'What do you mean?'

He knew something, or had worked something out, she was sure, but why was he being so cagey? Her feelings?

'In all the samples the parasite has reached a certain point in its growth before the host self-destructed.'

Jane thought about that and came up with an answer she suspected Chris was waiting for from her.

'Are you suggesting none of them were mature?'

He nodded.

Of course!

She quickly said, 'That would account for the lack of eggs or any other transmission vector. We haven't found out how it reproduces because we have yet to find an adult parasite. But how were these people infected?'

Chris was silent.

Carefully Jane said, ‘Carriers. There must be carriers of mature parasites that we haven’t come across yet. Perhaps one carrier who is aware of what he is, who wasn’t killed by the parasite, and all these,’ she gestured at the screen, ‘are the first to be infected.’

Chris studied her mildly. ‘That seems plausible.’

‘It would be nice to know how he survived the parasite’s growth,’ she said. She watched Chris uneasily. ‘How would we find this carrier, or these carriers?’

‘We know the parasite is an ETO.’

‘Somebody who has been off planet.’

‘That too, seems plausible.’

Chapter Five

The bank seals were no problem, since May had been provided with a chip card by one of the grey departments of World Health that should deal with them. Thoughtfully she pressed it home in its slot and waited. After a moment the lock issued a solid click and the card poked back out at her.

'Help me with this,' she told Carl and took hold of one side of the sealing bar.

'That's okay,' he said and lifted the bar from its dogs as if it was made of paper and propped it beside the door. She studied him speculatively, but could detect no sign of macho boastfulness.

'You're very strong,' she suggested.

He nodded his shaven head as if quite used to hearing this.

'Bring in the equipment,' she instructed him. 'Best to get set up as soon as possible. No telling when he'll be back.'

Carl nodded in acquiescence and headed back for the air car. May shook her head wonderingly, before inserting a skeleton key in the main door lock and quickly opening it. She stepped into the beach house, wrinkling her nose at the musty smell as she moved on inside. The interior was much as she expected: tastefully decorated and furnished, but a dusty and scattered here and there with black mildew from lack of occupancy. She studied her surroundings wondering where it would be best to set up the stun cannon and the wire guns. Shortly Carl returned carrying a heavy packing case.

'Put it down in the kitchen,' said May, wondering at his ability to take orders unquestioningly. Then he surprised her by asking a question.

'This will be sufficient to stop a man with cybernetic implants?'

'It ought to be. Do you know why we want him?' She was as yet unsure of what Carl knew, just as she was unsure of his rank.

'Something to do with illegal biologicals...'

He knew no more than her. She found this gratifying and at the same time rather worrying. She had been told that the subject was augmented, potentially very dangerous, and must be captured, put under maximum restraint and taken to headquarters. She knew no more than that.

It took very little time to set up the cannon and the wire guns, and once this was done May moved to the door.

'I'll go round the back now and short out the seals on any other doors. We don't want him coming in behind us. You set up the motion detectors.'

Carl nodded and smiled and May felt herself flush. He was damned attractive and so ... mild. She stepped out of the front door and set off along the slab path leading around to the back of the house. *Illegal biological.* She wondered precisely what they were to get World Health to take such steps as this. She had never been involved in an action without police sanction, and that worried her.

The single back door lay inside a conservatory in which much of the glass was broken. She climbed in through one of the windows and studied the seal. This was the test. She removed a second chip card and inserted it. The seal issued a loud buzz, then a click, and did not return the card. It had shorted, most certainly, but hopefully it had not set off an alarm in the local police station. She would not know whether or not it had until it was too late. Then ... movement caught her eye, and she peered through the tinted glass of the door into the kitchen and through the open front door. There were two people out there with Carl. For a moment she thought they might be the police, but surely they could not have got here so quickly. As quietly as she could she climbed out of the conservatory window and crept round the side of the house. As she drew nearer she heard voices.

'I must ask again who you are and what you are doing here?' asked Carl.

May waited nervously for the reply. For a moment there was silence, then a woman's dead voice replied, 'That is a question I must ask you.'

'Obviously you are not police. Or are the police being issued with proscribed weaponry now?'

A man's voice said, 'Two wire guns and a stun cannon. There are also ceramal restraints in the box.'

May crept to the corner of the house.

The woman said, 'You are working with World Health, I take it?'

Carl was silent.

'I will count to three then I will blow your leg off if you do not reply.'

Christ! Answer her Carl!

'One, two-'

May stepped round the corner. 'We are with World Health. There's no need for violence.'

The man and woman standing before Carl wore identical businesswear. They both had cropped blond hair and their emotionless features were nearly identical. May abruptly realised she had made the wrong move. These two had *killer* stamped all over them. The woman held a flat black pistol. The man held a portable anti-photon gun. May had only ever seen pictures of this weapon since mere possession of such was punishable by mindwipe and, in some countries, by physical death.

'Time to die,' said the woman, aiming her weapon at Carl.

Her gun made a burring sound and a stream of explosive micropellets blasted Carl back. May turned and ran, but the grass tangled her feet. She staggered, fell, rose again. There was no ceramal under her skin. The micropellets cut her in half.

Carl rose again with his ceramal chest exposed, synthetic skin and flesh hanging from him in burning tatters. The man turned, saw what he was, and instantly fired. *I cannot survive this* was Carl's last conclusion, and he began transmitting all he knew and all he was to his nearest counterpart. Purple fire ripped his world apart, hurling him back again and, as he fell, he glimpsed an air taxi in the sky doing a rapid U-turn and heading back towards the town. The fire then hit him a second time and his body, which could take being run over by a bulldozer, fragmented.

All that he was, all he had been...

The information hit Chris like a hammer, momentarily negating his motor functions so that he dropped the sample bottle he had been inspecting. The bottle smashed scattering sharp fragments along with a section of formalin-soaked parasite like wet cotton. He saw it with all of his heuristic function: glittering shards, spilled liquid, alien life. He was falling, but abruptly recovered, almost pulling the plug of the direct link from its socket in the back of his head. A wisp of smoke rose from the cable as he shunted everything he had been dealing with through the computer link over to autonomous function, while he consciously ran through the three-second burst.

Carl: *all that he was.*

In moments he had taken all he needed and boosted the remainder to the AI at World Health.

'Are you all right?' asked Jane, as if unsure that the question was relevant.

Chris was silent as decisions were made on a higher level and his instructions fed back to him. Then he gazed at Jane.

'They will probably try to kill you now,' he said.

'What?!' Jane almost dropped the sample bottle she was holding.

'There was information I was not allowed to pass on to you. I am now able to. One of my kind was destroyed. It is now imperative that the vector of the parasite be discovered and its source proven.'

'You're not making sense, Chris.'

'I will, but first we must leave here. We must find somewhere safe.'

Jane helplessly scanned her laboratory, her equipment, the work in progress.

'We must collect all that is necessary for your continued research,' Chris told her, 'all the records and all the samples. This place is no longer safe and may be destroyed. We must hurry.'

'Who wants to kill me?'

'TCC,' he replied bluntly. 'It was through them that the parasite was allowed onto Earth and now they seek to prevent this being known. Already two World Health operatives have been killed and an antiphoton weapon employed. These people are prepared to go to great lengths to cover their crime. We must hurry.'

Jane stared at Chris for a moment, concealing her qualms as he unplugged the direct link, pressed down the flap of syntheflesh on the back of his neck, then moved to the computer, coiling the cable as he went. It was not this sight of his other nature that got to her but that she had never heard him like this; never before heard such urgency. She set the computer to transfer all its records into a memory crystal while Chris collected up the samples. She felt panicked, but this did not impair her efficiency. Soon they had collected all the relevant data and samples and packed these in two attaché cases. And then they were outside, walking fast, nearly running.

The night was moonless with stars glinting as sharp as diamond fragments. A chill breeze was creaking the branches of the oak trees in the grounds and white dew lay heavy on the grass. Jane shivered and sneezed noisily as she headed for her aircar, but Chris caught her arm.

'No, too dangerous.'

Jane stared at him in confusion.

He glanced up at the sky. 'We must not be visible. It would be best for us to walk to the nearest taxi rank.'

'That's nearly three miles away,' said Jane almost in horror.

'It is best that we not be too visible.'

With chagrin Jane followed him out onto the overgrown road. Soon they were heading along a path trampled through the brambles, stinging nettles and sodden grass, wending their way between young trees that had grown twenty feet tall in the years since the tarmac had been scraped up. Jane clumped along muttering to herself, forgetting how only a few hours earlier she had been telling herself she must get some exercise. She felt like hell. Her cold had got worse, was probably turning into flu. A long ramble in the country was the last thing she needed.

‘I don’t see why we couldn’t use the car.’

Chris did not answer immediately, instead he came to a halt, turned and gazed back.

‘I think your answer is about to arrive,’ he said eventually.

Jane peered back as well, to the glow from the windows of her laboratory and the small flat beside it. For a moment she considered how she could be back there with her feet up and a glass of aquavit beside her. Then a ruby flash ignited the darkness. She averted her eyes, black shadows occluding her vision, just before Chris grabbed hold of her and pulled her to the ground. Damp grass pressed against her face. A sound ensued as of white-hot I-beams being dropped into water, then transformed into a rumbling explosion that turned the air above into a hot wind and filled it with burning oak leaves. The explosion seemed to grumble on for some time, but then halted abruptly, whereupon Chris allowed her to stand. Her laboratory and the flat beside it were now black skeletons filled with glowing embers, and the oak trees were burning. Suddenly Jane felt intensely sick. She did not want any aquavit now … perhaps later.

‘They will say it was a misfire, computer error, an accident, and it will be impossible to disprove. It will cost them millions in compensation, but not the billions in compensation the parasite would cost them,’ said Chris.

‘What the Hell was it?’ asked Jane tightly.

‘Satellite weapon, probably left over from one of the super-power’s old defence projects. TCC bought numbers of them to be converted for asteroid mining.’

'They would have seen the car and got it as well.'

Chris nodded.

'You knew this was going to happen?'

'It was probable,' said Chris. 'Their carrier escaped them. They are panicking now.'

Jane turned to him. 'Carrier?'

Chris nodded. 'His name is Jack Smith. He was the comet miner we spoke to him on the plane. I informed World health of his presence and they sent operatives to pick him up at his house, but they were killed by TCC killers – killers who used an antiphoton weapon they had intended to use on Jack Smith. There would have been no evidence left, just ashes.'

Jane bit back on the annoyance she felt at Chris for it would do her no good. He was a machine. Always she must remember that. 'Why didn't you tell me this from the start?'

'It was not seen as being immediately necessary that you know.'

Jane swore then angrily began to pull pieces of grass from her hair. She was uncomfortably aware that her nose was running and she did not have a hanky. She snuffled on her sleeve.

Chris added, 'That you know now is because of the danger to you.'

Summoning calm Jane asked, 'How did you find out about this Jack Smith and where is he now?'

'Before he suffered a convenient accident in a faulty space suit a doctor on the TCC space station informed us. We tried to pick Jack up but he lost us in Brazil. He is still lost to us, but hopefully not for long. Our apprehending him is what TCC fear.'

'Brazil.' Jane nodded. 'It was World Health that invited me to that conference just after you were assigned to me. I was manipulated right from that start.'

'Only because you are a good parasitologist.'

'What do we do now?'

'We stay in hiding until Jack Smith is found, then we move to confirm, on record, that he is the carrier, and have him tell us where, on record, he picked up the parasite.'

'Will that be enough evidence to fry TCC?'

'I do not know.'

'And what if he is not found?'

'I do not know,' said Chris, then he tilted his head and peered up into the sky.

Jane looked up there too in time to see a red star flare for a moment then fade. That was probably the satellite weapon TCC had used. They were again getting rid of incriminating evidence.

'What now?' said Jane, frowning at the sky.

'I do not know,' Chris repeated. After a moment they turned and walked into the night.

Chapter Six

Jack peered over the balcony rail down towards an ersatz stone well in which the hologram of a naked woman slowly writhed and smiled lasciviously. After a moment he looked up and scanned the other galleries and balconies, the shopping complexes, bars and cafes, all caught in crystal planes of mirror glass.

There.

The sign was the holographic depiction of a comet arcing in towards the sun, and of link mining ships like black spiders moving to intercept it. He allowed himself a smile, though in truth, after the events of the last couple of days, he really shouldn't feel much like smiling. After witnessing, from an aircab, that killing at his house, he knew some unpleasant characters were searching for him. Then there were the watchers at all the medscan facilities, some of whom certainly weren't undercover cops.

The bar was called 'The Comet Miner' – a now displaced profession. He could smile at that if at nothing else. He headed for the escalator and made his way there, finally coming to a door watched on either side by bouncers with fairly obvious cybernetic implants. They checked him over with a hand scanner, then allowed him to pass, probably supposing he was far too well-dressed to likely be a problem for them.

'Enjoy your evening, sir,' said the one with a cosmetically placed scar dividing his nose.

'I shall try to,' said Jack.

As he walked past them he felt the parasite poised inside him like a fist. Everywhere lay danger and the last two days had affected his unwelcome guest as well. At a slot machine inside he paid twenty Ecu for a UV transfer on his arm then followed the signs directing him to the main bar. Halson was there, drinking steadily and puffing on a Moroccan.

'Do you have what I require?' asked Jack, as he moved up to stand beside the man.

Halson glanced round, his pale unhealthy face in stark contrast to his helmet of black hair and neatly trimmed moustache.

'Jack Smith!' The greeting sounded forced. 'Have a drink.'

Jack slid onto a stool.

'Large Scotch for me,' he said, as Halson was buying.

The barmaid, a girl in a crevice-revealing body suit and balanced like a potential accident on spring-lift shoes, brought his drink to him before walking carefully to her next customer.

'Nice girl that,' Halson observed.

Jack nodded and dismissed the irrelevance. 'Do you have my tape?'

Halson nodded and turned his drink between his palms. Jack wondered if he had looked at the tape and was nervous now because he had seen the parasite. He took out his wallet, thumbed out two five-thousand Ecu notes and handed them over. Halson stared at the money as if he had been offered a severed hand, but then took it anyway.

Seated at his table with his gin-and-tonic before him, Saphron was clad like the epitome of the twentieth century English gentleman. He wore highly-polished brogues, a tweed suit, velvet waistcoat and old school tie. His dress however, was in stark contrast to his skull-like features, shaven head, and the five-inch chrome slug of a cerebral augmentation unit behind his left ear. Casually, he observed the three men and the woman seated at a table on the other side of the room overlooking the dance floor with its chaos of coloured light and moving shapes. He watched them, as they surreptitiously watched the two at the bar.

‘They have their mark,’ he subvocalized, appearing to take a sip of his drink. A voice replied to him directly through his augmentation.

‘Remote drones are all in place. Are they leaving yet?’

‘Not yet. Halson’s talking to the mark. Some sort of transaction going on there. The mark just handed over some high-denomination notes.’

‘We’ll pull Halson when they leave.’

‘Make it quiet. I don’t want them getting nervous. And be very very careful all round, all of you. Remember there’s still a proscribed weapon on the loose out there.’

That had really made his week; a crazy fucker demolishing seafront property with an APW.

‘Jethro’s in place inside up at the other bar. He’ll get Halson.’

Saphron gazed across at the cocktail bar. That was Jethro? The only other person standing there seemed to be a woman in a synthetic leather cat suit, but then, it was well known that Jethro would take on any job if it offered some chance of promotion.

As soon as the money had disappeared Halson reached into his top pocket and took out a small transparent cube the size of a die and handed it over. Still holding his wallet open Jack pressed the cube into the receiver of a small personal unit inside, then his fingers danced over the unit’s touch-plates. A small hologram sprang into life above the wallet and confirmed that this was indeed the recording he wanted. He touched the memorise plate then dropped his wallet on the bar and picked up his Scotch.

'You're recording it?' said Halson doubtfully.

Jack nodded.

'There are gigabytes of data in that crystal.'

'I know. But my unit should be able to handle it. The memory is fifteen terabytes.'

'Expensive.'

'Not really. I got it off of a colleague in Sao Paulo. He no longer had any use for it.'

A green glow ignited over the unit and Jack then hit the wipe pad. After a moment the cube rose out of its slot. It was now opaque. He slid the cube across the bar, pocketed his wallet and unit, and downed his Scotch.

'How?' said Halson, peering at the cube.

'Information acid,' said Jack. He felt a bit guilty about ruining all the formatting in the man's cube but did not trust him to erase its contents. It had been a sealed program, so he knew it had not been copied, but given time Halson could have found a way to break through that. Jack slid off his stool and, with a nod to Halson, headed for the door. He wanted out. The technician was acting strangely and the parasite lodging its protest.

'The mark's moving off now. Sune and her men are following. I'm on them.'

As Sune Jean's four thugs followed the man out of The Comet, Saphron stood up, his hand dropping to his jacket pocket and taking hold of a gun that was five millimetres thick and could easily have been mistaken for something out of a Christmas cracker, but which certainly was not. He was taking no chances this time. The last time he had run this kind of operation they had lost the mark and all but one of Sune's men.

Later, the mark had turned up on the market as bargain price spares. He had been an Olympic swimmer.

'They're heading down to ground level. Halson probably told them where he would be going. They'll probably take him outside the complex. Keep an eye out for a fast cruiser in the area.'

'We think we have it. It's a `47 Ford Macrojet. It's on its third circuit of the complex. We have two radar-dead drones on it.'

'Good work. Good work,' said Saphron, his mouth dry. 'They're coming to the street exit now. Keep on your toes.'

Jack's next awareness of danger was a violent stirring of the parasite. He turned and saw that three men and a woman had closed in behind him. The woman hesitated as he turned then stepped forwards raising a stun wand.

Weapon.

Suddenly the parasite poised in him like a scorpion oriented towards a threat.

No, damnit...

The wand issued a strobe flash of green light and Jack staggered back as the energy burst hit him in the chest like a shovel. Yet his recovery was nigh instantaneous. Like spring steel he jerked to a halt and shot forwards. His hand slapped and the stun wand exploded against the pavement. He chopped sideways, the edge of his hand an iron bar. A head broke and deformed and a man dropped as if he had stepped in a manhole. Jack smashed his forehead into the woman's face, hurling her back to the ground. He spun, side kicked, another man slammed against a wall where he seemed to stick for a minute before sliding down.

Oh shit shit shit!

Yet he kept moving.

The last of the four had retreated and was struggling to pull something from his pocket. He seemed to be moving in slow motion to Jack. Two fast paces and the heel of his hand came up like a hammer. The man went up and backwards crashing to the ground ten feet from where he had stood. His weapon went skittering across the pavement and dropped down a drain.

Jack came to a halt, a question mark of flesh and bone, death all around him. He glanced up at the sudden whine of a turbine and saw an aircar speeding away. With erratic birdlike movements he returned his attention to his attackers. Only the woman seemed to be alive. Jack wondered if she had been pretty. She wasn't now. He swallowed dryly, his throat clicking, now completely aware of what he had done, and more importantly, where. This was too visible and it was not Brazil. People were closing in, gaping at the scene, not ducking their heads and hurrying away. This would mean police and investigations and questions he would not want to answer. He turned and ran.

'Jesus Christ! Bring the drones in. Man running. Bring him down, fast. Possible illegal cybernetic implants!'

'What!?'

'The mark. He just wasted our four. He's heading for the old flood road, and fast! Jesus!'

Saphron sprinted to the four sprawled figures, glanced at the rapidly retreating figure, then looked up.

'And I want that aircar!'

'We're on it. Where's the mark now?'

'Gone, probably at the road by now.'

'Not another athlete?'

'Athletes don't move that fast.'

Before the induced flight reaction began to lapse Jack found himself on the old road across what used to be a flood plain before the new sea defences were built, with the town a mile behind him. He slowed to a walk, his every muscle a marble of pain as he gasped mechanically. As soon as he regained enough control, he turned to peer back towards the lights. From the shopping complexes he could see reflective objects spiralling up into the sky like fire flies. Security drones. He did not stand a chance. In minutes he would be found, and those drones carried stun cannons. The parasite did not know this though. It keyed into his fear reaction and boosted it. Before he knew what he was doing he was running again.

'Fugitive! Halt!' came a machine voice.

He ran harder, something crackling in his chest.

'Halt or ionic stun will be used!'

He felt the impetus to run faster but his body could no longer respond. His muscles were like stone and his breathing an accelerated panting. Suddenly a strobe flash cut through the air to him and knocked him sideways, pain convulsing his body, yet he stumbled on, a hot electrical smell in his nostrils. A panicked glance round showed him the drone like a hovering full-face crash helmet ten feet up from his right shoulder.

Enemy.

He glanced down, but there was nothing to hand he could use. He reached into his pocket just as the second shock hit him and sent him sprawling.

Enough enough enough!

Yet no matter his mental screaming he still took a fifty Ecu coin from his pocket, jerked upright, turned and threw.

The third shock threw him backwards with minor lightnings webbing his body. As blackness filled him he had the satisfaction of a subliminal glimpse of the drone limping through the air trailing sparks and smoke.

'You are aware, I should think, of the pointlessness of trying to lie? Your reactions are being monitored by a partial AI lie-detector, and not very much gets past that,' said Saphron smoothly.

Halson nodded and dipped his head, a bitter twist to his mouth.

'You are also aware of your rights, I should think, and are also aware, due to the seriousness of the crimes you have been involved in, that you do not have the right to remain silent. You may wait for your lawyer before we begin, though.'

Halson looked up, the bitter twist to his mouth becoming a strange grin. 'I'll tell you now. I've got nothing to lose any more. That bitch Sune used a genetic venom on me. I'm dead.'

Saphron blinked and accessed his augmentation for a confirmation of the pertinent information: genetic venoms were gene-specific, undetectable and required specific antivenins to neutralize them.

'What was your relationship with Jack Smith?' he asked, eventually.

Halson peered down at his knotted hands then across at the government sealed holocorder crouching up in the corner of the room like some weird insectile sculpture. 'He came to me for an unlogged medical scan. We get them quite often – people who fear they've picked up the latest strain of AIDS and don't want it reported, people on endorphins, people having trouble with illegal augmentations...' He trailed off with a glance at the aug on the side of Saphron's head.

'How is the medscan unit disconnected from World Health oversight?'

'It isn't. The scan is recorded into a sealed memory crystal provided by the client whilst simultaneously being sent to WH under a military security seal. Difficult to access.'

'I see. Tell me, what was the procedure once you had acquired this illegal scan?'

'The normal procedure would be to just hand over the crystal to the client and take the money.'

'Why didn't you follow this procedure?'

'Sune Jean.' Halson said the name as if he had a bad taste in his mouth.

'Tell me more.'

'I thought no one knew, but somehow she found out about it. A year ago I was dragged into an aircar and taken to her. She offered a set payment if I would provide her with information about any unusual scans: unusual eye colour, gland size, heavy nerve tissue, and other ... physical attributes. I refused. I knew what her game was and I didn't want to play. It was then that one of her thugs injected me with the venom. I had no choice.'

'What did you think her game was?'

'It was obvious. She was breaking people for parts – an organ thief.'

'We prefer the term murderer.'

'Yeah.'

'So tell me, what was the procedure in these cases?'

'Anything unusual and I got in contact with her. She named a place and I told the client that I could not pass the scan over at the facility and arranged to do so at the named place.'

'In Jack Smith's case this place was The Comet Miner?'

'Yeah.'

'Very well. What was unusual about Jack Smith?'

Halson suddenly looked nervous. 'He logged his tape in his personal unit. It was the only copy.'

'That does not answer my question.'

Halson looked up. 'Did you get him? Did you get Jack Smith?'

'That is not relevant.'

'Look at his unit. You find out. I've nothing more to say.'

'Interview closes 15:20.'

His first awareness was of confinement. He was lying down and straps held him. Immediately he began to struggle and something snapped with a sound like a gun shot. He had time then only to open his eyes and take in a room like a white prison cell before something bright and agonising flung him into blackness again.

His next awareness was of confinement too. He was in a chair. He struggled violently but to no result. It was as if he had been set in concrete up to his neck, yet his struggles did not cease until every muscle in his body became rigid with pain. Only then did he hear a voice and take note of his surroundings. The chair he sat in was in a cell. Ahead of him stood a door with an inset armour-glass portal at head height.

The voice droned on, 'Be calm. You are in a holding cell at Police Central Chelmsford pending interview. You will not be harmed. Be calm...'

Eventually the parasite relaxed its hold on him and sank back into wary somnolence. In time the door before him opened and in walked a man dressed in a tweed suit – a man with a cerebral augmentation unit on the side of his head. A woman in uniform came in behind and stood by the door.

'I must apologise for such undignified confinement Mr Smith, but when you first woke you broke your medical restraints then the arm of the nurse who was tending to you.'

'Free me,' said Jack in a hoarse voice he felt was his own, yet not. He could feel the parasite lurking around the edges of his mind ready to press the right button; to initiate or emphasise behaviour it considered would increase its survivability. Yet, that was wrong, he felt as if he was personifying something without sentience and reason, something that acted on a feral unconscious level, like instinct.

'Unfortunately, as a point of law, we cannot do that until whatever cybernetic implants you are carrying have been deactivated. This, as you may know, will probably take some time, so before I hand you over to the medtechs there are a few questions I would like you to answer.'

The man held Jack's own wallet in his hand, open to expose the personal unit, so it would not be long before he found out there were no implants. Jack nodded, not trusting himself to speak just yet. The parasite's imperative for freedom still influenced his actions just as the fear of pain prevented people from putting their hands in fire, yet it was more. Jack Smith wondered just who Jack Smith was.

'Before I go on,' said Saphron, 'is there anything you require?'

'Food, drink,' two more imperatives with possibilities inherent in having his hands free to eat and drink.

'Food and drink will be brought to you, but for obvious reasons you will have to be fed.'

Jack bowed his head.

Saphron nodded to himself. 'Firstly, I understand that you recently arrived from Brazil. Is that correct?'

Jack nodded.

'Upon your arrival you deposited a large sum of money with Ecubank and claimed the key card to the bank seals on your house on the sea wall?'

Again Jack nodded.

'Shortly after this your house was destroyed by an APW and an unidentified woman was found shot dead nearby.'

Jack's head jerked up. 'I ... knew nothing of this.'

'We have a statement from the driver of an air taxi telling us that she was taking you out to your house when the event occurred, and that you directed her to take you back to Maldon.'

Jack remained silent.

'Whatever, we will get to the bottom of this. I do not like bodies or illegal weaponry, and both of these seem to proliferate around you Jack Smith. Now tell me. What was the reason for this medscan?' He held up the wallet in his left hand and tapped the personal unit with his right forefinger. 'Is it drug-related or to do with your implants?'

Jack thought quickly. 'My implants. I've been having rejection problems.' It was a lie that would have a short life, he knew. He had to escape. The parasite seemed to writhe within him. He felt sick with adrenaline and the agonising urge to urinate.

Saphron continued, 'The recording in this unit will either prove or disprove that, but be assured you will not be leaving this place until I have some satisfactory answers.'

'Lawyer. I want a lawyer.'

'Yes,' said Saphron, 'it would seem you already have one. Your record shows that you are still a de facto employee of TCC and as such entitled to one of their lawyers. They have been informed.'

As Saphron left, Jack bowed his head again, trying to understand the sudden panic he felt. Later, a nurse came and fed him soup as if he were a baby. The parasite remained quiescent and he was able to talk to her relatively coherently. He asked to be freed to go to the toilet. She told him of the vacuum toilet in the chair. The chair was his prison.

They were closer than twins, cloned from the most successful CIA killer of the previous century, speed grown in the same tank, base programmed by the same synaptic computer, and finish-trained by a genius in the arts of death. One of them had undergone a sex-change operation in infancy, because as a pair it was considered they would be more closely bonded this way. The Toad had paid a small fortune for them and considered it well spent, until now.

'He escaped you and he is now in the hands of the police. How do I know this? I know this because of a memo from our legal branch. And what do you know? He is somewhere in Essex!' The hologram gesticulated violently and rose an embarrassing distance out of its chair. The Toad was obviously in his quarters near the centre of the TCC satellite, quarters he always seemed to move to when he felt threatened. It was the blank-faced woman who replied to him.

'Another satellite strike would negate the threat.'

'I see. I have had twelve of my best technicians killed and a satellite destroyed all to make a cover story of terrorists and incompetence and you suggest that I let another eighty million dollar satellite go the same way. You suggest that I permit a strike on Police Central in Chelmsford. Idiot! If I want suggestions I'll ask an AI not a moronic killer!'

'What do you require of us?'

The Toad sat forwards. 'I require that you kill Jack Smith and destroy the evidence that his body contains. You will await instructions. Somehow you will get into Police Central. It is not important whether or not you get out again.'

'We understand.'

'Oh good... You will be contacted.'

The hologram flickered out.

The screen showed the image of a man of glass; glass arms and legs, torso and head, glass organs veins and bones.

'Augment intrusions,' said the ginger-haired girl.

The picture flickered a couple of times and a shimmering bar code appeared at the bottom of the screen. A scan line ran up and down the image of the man a number of times.

'What's happening?' asked Saphron, leaning on the desk beside her.

'Difficult to say, sir. I get this every time I ask for the augmentations to be highlighted. It's as if the computer is having difficulty separating them from the rest of his body. This could be because of the sheer extent of his … augmentations. Ah, here we are.'

Suddenly the man-image filled with red strands, as if stuffed with red hot wire wool. These strands coalesced in a thick red rope enwrapping his glassy vertebrae.

'What's this, more glitches, it looks like a view of his nervous system. I want to see the implants.'

'There are none, and this is not a glitch.'

'I beg your pardon?'

'If this recording is correct there are no cybernetic implants, and it would appear that Jack Smith is the host for some kind of organism ... sir.'

'It's alive?'

The ginger-haired girl nodded.

Saphron stood upright, pulled another chair from under the table then sat down. 'I've had drug runners, body breakers, illegal weapons, murder and manslaughter this month. This I don't need. You're sure?'

'If you are sure it's from a genuine medscan facility and has not been altered, sir.'

'I'm as sure as I can be, given the suspects and witnesses. We'll have to give Smith another scan to check...' He trailed off and stared at the screen.

'Sir, this organism is probably some form of parasite. If such is the case then it has to be reported.'

'I know,' Saphron snapped, 'World Health must be informed immediately.' Still he sat there, gazing at the image.

'In fact, sir, I took the liberty, as you were busy...'

Saphron gaped at her as if she had suddenly grown horns. She went on, 'They are sending a Professor Jane Ulreas and her assistant Chris Golem.'

'Thank you, Jennifer. Your competence has been noted.'

There was a knock at the door and Jane felt her insides tighten. Could this be..?

'Chris here.'

The tightness receded, thankfully. She headed over to the door, then paused. Could it be that someone had copied Chris's voice and just replayed it? No, damn it. Being scared was one thing and sliding into paranoia another. She unlocked the door and jerked it open, stepping back as Chris entered the motel room.

'Any news?' she asked.

'Lots. It would seem that TCC are claiming that one of their weapons was taken over by terrorists. That flare we saw shortly after your laboratory was hit was the weapon and those manning it being destroyed by a missile from the TCC station itself.'

'Manning it?'

'Yes. No doubt it will be claimed they were criminals acting without the knowledge of TCC.'

'Will TCC get away with it?'

'They would have if that action had been the only one they had taken, but evidence is mounting against them. It is not an action they will be able to take again.'

'Bastards! What about my lab?'

'No doubt TCC will pay the bill as a sign of good faith.'

Irony? No, of course not.

'That, I suppose, is if I am still alive to accept the damages.'

'I am sure that is something they would like to correct.' He paused, 'There is also some other news.'

'Tell me about it. I'm sure things can't get any worse.'

'Jack Smith was apprehended by the police yesterday. He was apparently involved in some criminal activity during which some people were killed. He was confined under suspicion of carrying illegal cybernetic implants. The parasite was subsequently discovered in him and World Health informed.'

'Why? Why were you informed?'

'It is standard police procedure in the case of what might be illegal biologicals.'

'What do we do now?'

'Now we go and see Jack Smith. Once you have made an examination of him and that examination is on record you will be safe. TCC will have no reason to get rid of you. Expert testimony can be pre-recorded for the trial.'

‘But I have to make that examination and testimony.’
‘There are few other options open to you.’

Chapter Seven

He woke from blackness to razor clarity. Whilst using the catheter and special vacuum toilet in the chair and felt a dull anger at his restraints. They knew now that he had no implants, and they knew about the parasite, but did that merit such undignified treatment? He took a deep breath and closed his eyes, subdued the anger, opened his eyes. Then he considered escape with *all* of his mind.

The room was four-point-two metres square with a ceiling two metres high. He knew this in a glance. Estimations of measurements flashed through his mind. Side-tracked for a moment, he measured the chair with his eyes and guessed at its structure and of what alloys it must be constructed, then he fixed his eyes on the door. Ceramal plate over aluminium honeycomb, electric bolt locks at the top and bottom. He focused on the plate, his vision close up, as through a magnifying glass. He searched for weaknesses and found them. He estimated it would take him about twenty seconds to get through. Again he fixed his attention on the chair, but here there seemed to be no weaknesses he could work on. It was over-engineered; strong enough to hold someone with four times the strength of a normal man. Just strong enough.

When he had finally gone over the room and all it contained inch by inch, he turned his attention inward and considered what he might say to his captors. As he thought about this, another part of his mind continued to calculate and those calculations slewed off into the bizarre. In a flicker of thought that lasted a picosecond he realized what he was doing and was exhilarated. Then he decided to test this new found ability.

Still with two thinking processes in action Jack began simultaneously to recall events in his near and far past. He had complete recall. He pushed his mind, ran through five separate events and made calculations on those events; the probable force of a blow, the angle of ricochet of a bullet and its probable speed, the likely thoughts passing through a woman's mind, the temperature and position of the sun, the date, the position of certain comets on that date. He was amazed at what he knew; facts picked up by reading, from a glance at a holovision in a shop window, from the back of a cereal packet.

He also felt a strange dread when he found he could not plumb the depths of this clarity of thought and drew a line beyond which he would go only when necessary. As he drew that line he realised why he could think like this: the parasite. To it his body was a tool for its own survival and his brain was part of that tool. It had improved the function of his brain just as it had improved the function of the rest of his body. He understood that he was not under any more direct control than a normal person is by the imperatives of survival. His actions had been controlled by his own mind; instinctive, unconscious. The parasite was using his mind for what it did best: for thinking. It was not controlling his thoughts. This was just another aspect of the parasite's growth and had been going on for some time. How else had he managed to control his parasite-augmented body?

A terrible clarity and nuance of meaning infected his thoughts and seemed to recur to infinity, yet it did not make him unhappy. What had he been before but a slavish machine for the passing on of his own genes? Now he was a slave to the parasite ... and he was the parasite, or was that the right word? Was the right word now symbiosis, mutualism, or should there be any kind of separation at all?

None, he realized. *I am the parasite.*

Jack leant his head back against the headrest and felt at one with himself. It was almost a religious experience, though perhaps it had more contentment than such. A deep calm filled him and from that calm he gazed out again and viewed his situation. He studied the chair again, inspected the bracing that held his arms. *What is the extent of my control over my body? How much stronger could I make one arm?*

Jack tried to lift his arm. There was no movement. He concentrated and threw all his strength into it. The chair creaked. He increased the pressure until sweat broke out on his forehead and his muscles were burning.

Something cracked.

He was getting angry. He knew it was the wrong thing to do, but he could not help himself. For too many years he had seen the trail of broken bodies and grief this woman had left behind her and was too involved. He abruptly turned away from the table and faced the wall whilst he tried to get himself under control. *Sune Jean Rhienz, I could kill you now without the slightest regret.* He turned back to the table.

The plastiskin on Sune Jean's face was a source of infinite satisfaction to Saphron. He regretted that they still had to hold Jack Smith in custody. The man deserved his freedom.

'Okay, we'll forget about the other victims for a moment. The scanner technician Halson claims one of your men injected him with a genetic venom.'

'Genetic venom? What's that?'

'Don't fuck me about. Even if you are as innocent as you claim you would know what a genetic venom is. You have the qualifications.'

'Ah yes,' Sune Jean leant forwards, put her elbows on the table, and began to toy with her plastic cup. Chinese water torture. 'I think ... I recollect now. It's been such a long time since I took my doctorate... Gene specific ... venoms tailored to an individual's genetic code. They're very difficult to trace and the antivenins are almost impossible to make unless, of course, you were the one who tailored the venom. Am I right?'

'You know you are.'

'Really?'

'We want you to give us the formulation of the venom you gave Halson.'

'I thought you said one of my men gave it to Halson.'

'Don't play semantics with me!' Saphron cracked his hand down on the table. The plastic cup leapt into the air, its dregs spilling in a small pool. Sune Jean watched the cup expressionlessly as it rolled off the table. Saphron glanced at the officer at the door, then stepped back.

'There will be certain benefits for you if you give us this formulation.'

Sune Jean began to write in the spilt tea. 'If, as you say, I am guilty of the crimes you have described, I cannot see what benefits there could be. One death more or less would not alter the penalty ... the ultimate sanction of the law...'

Saphron felt a horrible coldness. She just did not care. He should have realized this from her indifferent response when he asked her if she wanted a lawyer present.

'I suppose I would be wasting my time if I appealed to your better nature?'

Sune Jean glanced up at him and smiled, then dipped her head down again and continued to doodle strange and curious shapes in the tea. Saphron turned away and and slammed out of the room. 'Bitch, bloody bitch!'

'Er, sir...'

Saphron glanced around and saw that Jennifer, his secretary, was standing next to him. He noticed how pretty she was, just like Sune Jean had been before Jack Smith smashed her face. Strange how meaningless exteriors could be.

'What is it? What do you want?'

'Two representatives of World Health have arrived: Professor Jane Ulreas and Chris Golem. They're waiting in your office.'

Saphron glared at the door to the interrogation room holding Sune Jean. Perhaps this was what he needed; something else to do, some time to distance himself again. He nodded and set off down the corridor, Jennifer tagging along behind like an anxious terrier.

'Chief Inspector Saphron,' he said as he finally entered his office.

The two people sitting before his cluttered office turned to watch him, creepily in complete harmony. So, these were Professor Jane Ulreas and Chris Golem – two people with entirely different names. Yet, with their identical grey suits, cropped blond hair, their shared stillness and the lack of expression on their very similar faces, they could have been twins.

The blank-faced woman stood up. 'It is imperative that we see Jack Smith immediately,' she said.

The blank-faced man stood up also, reaching down to pick up a heavy briefcase.

After an hour he had to desist, feeling drained and his arm like bruised meat in a tin. When, shortly after that, a nurse came to him, a sure sign his condition was known amongst the medical staff of the station, he realized he was now a patient as well as a prisoner. The nurse brought him a sparse meal of soup and bread. He swore at her.

'Now Mr Smith there's no need for that.'

'Prison fare, is that it? Bread and water?'

'We didn't think you would want—'

'I'm hungry,' he said, and he was.

'I'll see what can be done,' she said, standing.

Abruptly he altered his tone. 'Sorry, not your fault. I guess they gave you no instructions concerning extra nutrition. The parasite you know...'

She looked uncomfortable. Her lips formed into an *oh*. He knew there would have been no such instructions and he did not want her to check. He gave her his most sincere smile.

'I need a high protein and sugar diet else there's a chance I'll go into coma.' He noted to himself there the pun about comets before he went on, 'At the moment I'm pretty depleted. I need a quantity of glucose drinks, high solution – a litre or so – and something like eggs or steak. Can you get that for me?' He smiled again.

The nurse continued to stare at him as if hypnotised. Jack realized he was listening to her heartbeat and the rhythm of her breathing. He saw then what he had been doing on an unconscious level and brought it to consciousness. He changed his tone and continued to speak, fixing her gaze with his and moving his head slightly from side to side.

'You'll get these for me. Yes, you will won't you? Plenty of glucose drinks, perhaps more than a litre? Two litres? Three litres? You'll be the best judge of that of course. And eggs, don't forget the eggs. A dozen eggs. Raw. You can break them into the drinks. Yes, that would be best. Hurry back.'

The nurse turned away, shaking her head as if she had passed through cobwebs. Her palm against the panel by the door opened it for her and she was soon gone. Jack closed his eyes. He was shaking. *What am I?* The answer came to him in a hundred ways in shouts and whispers.

The nurse returned in less than twenty minutes and in a daze she fed him three litres of a saturated solution of glucose with raw eggs broken into it. As he gulped Jack could feel his stomach distending and when he had finished he could feel it emptying. Energy flowed into him like an adrenaline rush.

'You may leave now.'

The nurse stood and turned for the door.

'Wait.' Jack paused. He had been about to ask her to leave the door open but decided he had better not push his luck. There were limits. He knew, for example, that there was no way she would release him from the chair. 'Thank you,' he said, instead.

The nurse smiled and went on her way, closing the door behind her. Immediately Jack concentrated on his right arm. The burning was like acid in his veins, the force of his arm that of a hydraulic ram, and the sound of cracking ceramal, angelic music. He peered down at his arm, released now. It was swollen and bruised yet only flesh. *What am I?* He wondered yet again. And as he went on to junk the chair he said to himself, 'Jack Smith.' It was the only answer that sufficed.

Saphron ignored their obvious anxiety to get to Jack Smith and headed for sanctuary behind his desk. He noted that Jennifer had followed him in and was waiting by the door, her expression perplexed. He was about to tell her to leave, then changed his mind since this was her area after all and she would be working with these two, no doubt.

Once seated, he took a moment to arrange some papers and position his note screen. It was a bureaucratic pause – a way of asserting authority.

'Please sit down,' he said, in his most peremptory tone. The two looked at each other. Silent agreement seemed to pass between them. They sat.

'Now, why this great anxiety to see Jack Smith? We have him in confinement and the situation is under control. And hopefully, I have no great need to remind you that you are here in an advisory capacity.'

As always it was the woman who spoke. 'The parasite as described by your colleague is the reason for our haste. It was first discovered in Brazil–'

'Brazil?' Saphron interrupted. 'That ties in. This Jack Smith recently flew over from there. Do go on.'

'The problem with this parasite is that we do not as yet know how it is transmitted or infectiousness it might be. In the interests of everybody's health we must first determine if it is the same parasite and then bring about suitable quarantine ... precautions.'

Saphron nodded affably. What she said made sense, yet there was something here that did not quite gel. He was unsure about these two, so pulled over his note screen, accessed the Internet and casually he began to make inquiries.

'It would seem this parasite has some pretty strange effects on its host,' he said. 'We thought he had cybernetic implants. It took a number of stuns from a remote drone to bring him down and he still managed to scrap it with a fifty–'

There was a *phut* like the sound of someone swatting a fly.

Saphron glanced up in time to see Jennifer jerk back, hit the door, bounce and sprawl on the floor. Blood pumped out of the wet hollow in the back of her head. Saphron stared at her without comprehension for a moment then slowly turned to face the blank-faced woman. She held a small silenced pistol pointed rigidly at his forehead.

'You will lift your hands very slowly away from that note screen. You will not press one more key.'

There was a key that lay half an inch from his little finger under a flip cap. Two seconds and alarms would be blaring and armed police battering their way into this room. Saphron well knew that the distance between his forehead and the evil black eye of that gun could be travelled by a bullet in so much less time than two seconds. He lifted his hands up into the air.

'Why? Why did you kill her?'

'She realized. It was obvious. She was also excess baggage.' The woman glanced at her partner and nodded at the still quivering body on the floor. The man stood, walked over and picked up the corpse in one hand, dragged it to concealment one side of Saphron's desk.

'What do you want?'

'You will come out from behind that desk, very carefully. My brother will search you. Should you attempt anything stupid my brother will break your hands.'

As he stood up and moved to obey Saphron said, 'You don't work for World Health, I take it.' In any other situation that comment might have been humorous, but the blood and the brains on the floor and the warm corpse hunched by his desk were not the best elements of comedy.

'You are most observant.' Irony negated by her blank expression. While her brother searched Saphron thoroughly and professionally, she continued, ‘Shortly you will lower your hands to your sides and take us to Jack Smith’s cell. Should you attempt anything stupid my brother will break your hands.’

Like robots, thought Saphron, using the same phrase with same meaning, and feeling no need to change it for aesthetic purposes. He lowered his hands as her brother backed away from him, frustrated as a pen spring under a brick. He noted that, as she stood, the barrel of the woman’s gun wavered not one millimetre from its aim at the centre of his forehead. It could have been fixed there with a steel rod.

‘Now, open the door and wait. When you are tapped on the shoulder, advance into the corridor three paces. When you hear the door close behind you, you may continue on to the cell block. Incidentally, we know where the cell block is and the security procedure for getting in there. The latter is the reason you are still alive.’

Saphron opened the door and stepped out into the corridor. The door closed behind him and he advanced with sweat slick on his back. It frightened him more than he liked to admit that he could not hear them walking behind him. Halfway down the corridor, the woman spoke again.

‘My weapon is now concealed, but it would be best for you understand that I can draw it and fire it faster than you can turn. This though, would not be necessary. My brother could break your neck even faster.’That flat emotionless voice was almost as frightening as the silence.

At the end of the corridor Saphron turned right. A secretary came out of an office holding a box of memory crystals, and nodded and smiled at him as she passed. Saphron wondered what he would do if they came upon an armed officer, sentence him to death? As it transpired they reached the barred doors to the cell block without event.

'Place your hand on the palm lock. When the door opens continue on to Jack Smith's cell.'

Saphron nodded, then placed his hand on the square to one side of the door and it slid open with a quiet hiss. He advanced. Excess baggage, that's what she said. He realized with growing horror that, as soon as he opened the door to Jack Smith's cell, he would become just that. The cell lay ahead of him, there, to the right. He had to do something.

'I–' he began, and jerked to one side as he said it. With a loud crash the door to Jack Smith's cell hit the opposite wall. The pistol fired twice as Saphron dropped to the floor and rolled. As he came up in a crouch, ready to run, he just froze in shock seeing the armoured door thump down in the corridor. What the hell? He glanced at the two killers, realizing he had missed the chance to act. *I'm dead*, he thought, but the two were ignoring him.

'Now!' shrieked the woman. 'The APW!'

Oh shit! Saphron put his arms over his head as an empty briefcase hit the floor beside him. An actinic purple flash took his vision away momentarily, yet in the moment of that flash he thought he saw a shape moving impossibly fast. A tremendous explosion shook the building. Saphron felt himself lifted from the floor by shock wave, his ears ringing, masonry falling all around him, the smell of burning plastic in his nostrils. The corridor filled with dust as he tried to blink back his vision. Finally he saw the male killer's feet before his face, the APW lying junked beside them, then he glanced up and saw, as the man toppled, that he had no head. A voice impinged then over the ringing in Saphron's ears.

'I understand now. So clear. TCC allowed me to get away with the memory crystals to avoid quarantine restrictions on that last load of ice. It's so obvious. Now they are in trouble.

For that small amount of profit they gambled billions and now they are losing. I suppose they did not see it that way. The parasite I carried then was a small risk.'

Saphron rolled over to a sight that warmed his heart. Jack Smith had one hand around the woman's throat, pinning her against the wall with her feet off the ground. He seemed oblivious to the fact that her face was turning blue.

'It could be said then that I am the only tangible evidence against them, or rather, against the Toad ... is that not so?' Abruptly he noticed the woman's condition and lowered her to the ground. But as she gasped for breath he did not release his hold.

'You are a killer employed by TCC. Not too bright though. You're still dressed in TCC businesswear. No matter.' He stopped to consider for a moment, then continued. 'You won't be the last. Whilst I remain a threat to him the Toad will continue to send killers after me until I am dead.'

'We can get them,' said Saphron, then coughed the dust from his throat.

Jack deigned to notice him. 'I think not, Detective Inspector Saphron. I doubt that there is enough evidence against TCC or the Toad, and even if there is enough evidence the legal branch of TCC will tie up the courts for the next century. No. The Toad must be brought to book another way. I feel a personal affront.'

'But–' Saphron got no further. Jack's hand jerked up and twisted with a horribly gristly crunch, the woman gagging, her legs kicking. Then in a moment Jack was gone, even before the woman hit the floor to make her last futile spastic attempts at life. Saphron felt no inclination to assist her.

Chapter Eight

'Flight sector 16.23 east is closed to all aerial traffic. This sector is for use of emergency services only. If you wish to enter this sector please approach the ground cordon. This is a recorded message. Flight sector –'

The driver switched off the radio while the aircab hovered by drone emergency lights dotted round the sky in a three mile cylinder above Chelmsford Police Central.

'What now? You wanna go down by the cordon?'

Jane stared at Chris with dawning horror. However, she was not distracted from taking another large bite of her burger.

'They couldn't have. They wouldn't have,' she said round a mouthful of woolly bread and unidentifiable meat.

Chris appeared thoughtful for a moment then said, 'They didn't. No satellite weapons have been used. Probably a bomb or that APW. We have to find out.' He turned to the perplexed driver and said, 'Take us down to the cordon.'

The aircab spiralled down past the drone lights and came to hover over a street filled with gawking crowds held back by electric barriers and police in riot gear. The driver surveyed the situation for a moment then took them down behind the crowds.

'Looks like some sort of a show going on there. Probably the New Luddites again, seems their kind of action.' When no comment was forthcoming from his passengers he fell silent until they had landed. 'Here we are.' Chris handed his card over for the charge, retrieved it, then he and Jane got out of the cab.

‘The man we want to see is a Detective Inspector Saphron, spelt with a ph.’

In a moment they were pushing through the crowds. Chris was very good at this. If people did not get out of the way he gently but firmly lifted them up and deposited them to one side. Shortly they stood at the edge of the crowd. Between that edge and the electric barrier there lay a respectful gap. Beyond the barrier a group of riot police stood drinking coffee and chatting, stun rifles tucked under their arms, and beyond them a heavy fire engine was heaving itself into the sky.

‘Come on,’ said Chris. He advanced to the barrier and with a crackle and sparks shorting around his feet into the ground lifted a section to one side. They stepped through. ‘It might be advisable for us to raise our arms right now.’ They did so just as the riot police caught sight of them and brought their weapons to bear.

‘On the ground! Lie down!’ shouted one of the officers.

‘That will not be necessary. We are here to see Detective Inspector Saphron. We have identification.’

There was a flash, Chris stumbled back and, Jane thought, deliberately fell over. She got down on the ground just as fast as she could and looked aside at him. He winked at her.

‘They seem a little nervous today.’

Humour; there was no doubt. The machine was a bloody comedian. She was still hungry and now she had a stinking headache.

‘Cuff them,’ said the officer who had fired the shot, and in a moment they were dragged to their feet, their hands secured behind them, and marched to Police Central. Chris, of course, was groggy and kept stumbling. He did not want to scare these poor misguided officers.

In retrospect the Toad wished he had listened to Bannerman and quarantined Jack Smith, his ship, and that load of complex ice. The sums were quite simple. The profit from that load of ice had amounted to five hundred and seventy-six million Ecu, approximately. The hunt for Jack Smith and necessary cover-ups thus far, including the destruction of a satellite weapon, had cost TCC one thousand seven hundred and eighty-six million Ecu, with a potential five hundred million yet to pay, but only if the origin of the parasite was not discovered. However, these huge amounts of money detracted not one wit from the Toad's comfort. It was the stock holders who would feel the pinch, not him. It was a pinch of another sort he feared.

Gaol. The word filled him with an emotion he had not felt in years and which seemed well able to ruin his digestion. He had not been able to drink brandy now for two whole weeks, and his usual Stilton and prawn jacket potato brunch was out of the question. Milk and water biscuits were the staple of his diet now. It was intolerable. He had just about done all he could and still there was a strong possibility that he would be summoned to Earth. Intolerable. He peered up at the ceiling.

'Lilly, have Stroud, Mendelssohn and Mason arrived yet?'

An impersonal woman's voice replied, 'Only Stroud and Mason so far, sir. I am having difficulty tracing Mendelssohn.'

'Send them in then and inform me as soon as you have the whereabouts of Mendelssohn.'

He sat back in his chair and glanced to either side at the holocameras mounted on the walls. He did not want to miss one detail of this. He was a perfectionist and this time he wanted things to go off without a hitch. It was still a source of annoyance to him that the doctor, Bannerman, had managed to knock aside one of the holocameras during his big exit so that a whole angle of view was lost to the Toad. This time it would be right.

After a moment the doors to his office slid open and a young hard-faced man and an old woman entered.

'My dear Rebecca, David.'

Rebecca Mason studied the Toad with deep suspicion. David Stroud nodded his head in a perfunctory but business-like manner. He had a file tucked under one arm and his businesswear was immaculate, whilst she wore a blue coverall, which was standard dress in the Bioscience departments. All she carried was a plastic walking stick, which in the Toad's inner office she did not really need.

'Please, be seated,' said the Toad congenially.

They moved forwards and occupied two of the three form-following armchairs before the Toad. The armchairs altered their shapes to suit, almost engulfing the two.

'Now, I've called you here because we have a little bit of a problem,' said the Toad.

'An understatement I think,' said Rebecca.

The Toad glared at her in annoyance before continuing.

'Obviously, when Bannerman informed us of this parasitic ETO we considered it of comparatively minor importance. Then,' he regarded Rebecca pointedly, 'it was the belief of Bioscience that Jack Smith would die without passing it on or that it would be taken as an Earth parasite, with no connection to us, which, of course, was why we only allowed him access to the shuttle going down in South America.'

'A particularly worm-ridden place,' interjected Rebecca, 'we may still be able to force that issue.'

'No, unfortunately not. It would seem that most authorities are coming to agree that it is an ETO. But allow me to continue.' The Toad turned his attention to David Stroud.

'World Health were informed by Bannerman of the situation. A lapse in security I find unacceptable, with a consequent cost I find unacceptable. There are few options left open to us now. Obviously, Jack Smith must be eliminated. That is of paramount importance. I have also ordered that all evidence which connects us with this imbroglio be deleted from our files, even so far as evidence that Jack Smith even worked for us. All his old associates are now on long range missions. Many of them will not come back. Others have been silenced by whatever means I deemed necessary, be that money or … otherwise.'

He paused and carefully studied the two before him as if expecting them to add something. When they said nothing he continued. 'World Health is preparing to take us to court. As far as I can see they will have great difficulty proving anything. Some of our experts in the legal and finance departments inform me that we should be able to keep this in the courts for a very long time at not even one per cent of the cost of compensation.'

'One per cent,' said Stroud, and gave a low whistle. 'What are the projected compensation costs?'

The Toad said, 'Right now they are at over a billion Ecu, but that is only for Brazil, most of which we own. With the parasite now spreading to some of the more wealthy countries it is estimated that the figure will double every year unless a ... cure is found.'

Rebecca said, 'As you said, limited options, what more can be done? What do you want us to do?'

'Well there is, in fact, nothing more for you to do. As I see it, it is the incompetence of both of you that has put us in this situation.'

'Now wait a minute–' began Stroud, but Rebecca interrupted him.

'Shut up, Stroud. Do go on, Geoffrey.' With great care she picked up her cane and put it across her lap.

'Dear Rebecca,' said the Toad, 'I had that cane of yours disarmed a month ago.' He stood up. As he did so David Stroud tried to stand as well.

'I ... I can't get out of my seat.'

Rebecca now tried to stand. Her face went white. She raised her cane and pointed it at the Toad, depressed a stud on its side, but nothing happened. The Toad grinned.

'The chairs, you will have noted, have gripped you round the lower halves of your bodies. Your breathing will not be constricted. Now that you are sitting comfortably I have some films to show you. The first is of a certain Doctor Bannerman's heroic attempts to put on a space suit. The ones that follow have a cast that include a number of Jack Smith's colleagues and friends. It is a very unusual collection, but not, as yet, complete. The last film is to be of two people being crushed to death in hydraulic armchairs. The sound of cracking pelvises will be so realistic. The screaming will be poignant. You are honoured. You are to become art.'

The burger vendor gaped at Jack with something approaching awe as he handed over the tenth double cheeseburger and milk-shake. Jack paid and returned to his table. He wondered what that man would think if he knew that this was the third place he had been in today. He estimated that he had put on about two stones of weight and when he looked in a mirror now he noted that his face was beginning to look a bit less skeletal. That would change though. He was only over-fuelling himself in preparation, but for what? How the hell did one go about stowing away on a space shuttle? Of course he could have bought a ticket like anyone else, but he suspected that as soon as

TCC security found out he was aboard the shuttle, it would have been involved in a tragic accident. There had to be another way.

As he munched into his burger he considered everything he knew about TCC operational procedures. By the time he was wiping the grease from his lips with a tissue he knew how it could be done. He needed a space suit, access to a TCC cargo, and a piece of software that could only be acquired from a professional smuggler. He stood and left the cafe.

'So you two really are Jane Ulreas and Chris Golem?' said Saphron, dabbing at his bloody nose.

'Yes, we are,' said Jane, 'and we have identification.'

'What?'

'We have identification,' said Chris in a substantially louder voice.

Saphron leant back against the ambulance and watched as two corpses were stretchered out of Police Central. His expression was all grim satisfaction. After a moment he gestured to the escort of riot police.

'You can take their cuffs off. These two really are who they claim. I checked that out.'

The cuffs were removed and Jane rubbed at her wrists in relief.

'What happened here?' Chris asked, his voice still loud.

'Poetic justice. Poetic bleeding justice,' said Saphron. He seemed not to have heard Chris as he stepped past them and went to one of the stretchers, now ready to be loaded onto the ambulance. They followed up behind him as he pulled a sheet back. Underneath lay the corpse of a woman with medical plastiskin on her face. Another two stretchers arrived while he was studying her. He glanced round at Chris and Jane.

'This one is a woman called Sune Jean Rhienz.' He then pointed. 'That is one of her associates. They both died when the cell block collapsed.' He now pointed to the two new stretchers. 'Those two claimed to be Professor Jane Ulreas and Chris Golem.'

'Killed in the cell black collapse too?' asked Jane.

'No, Jack Smith got them before they got him. I cannot tell you how good it makes me feel to see these four here like this.' Saphron dropped the sheet and turned fully to face Jane and Chris. 'There are things I want you to tell me. We'll go inside. At least the administrative section of the station is still standing.'

They entered the main entrance of Police Central through a foyer swamped two-inches deep with fire-retardant foam. Saphron led them up some stairs and, after trying a couple of doors, found an unoccupied office. There he ensconced himself behind a desk while they pulled up a couple of chairs.

'Okay, what the Hell is going on?' He did not bother with the shuffling of papers this time.

Jane looked to Chris. 'I think I'll leave it to you. I'm out of my depth.'

Chris nodded and began to speak in his smoothly modulated voice. 'Approximately three years ago the last comet mining operation came to an end. It ended with a ship load of comet ice brought from the Planc 12 comet. The pilot of that ship was a certain Jack Smith.'

Jane sat back in her seat. This was going to be a long one, but she wanted to hear the whole thing told just as much as the Detective Inspector did. And she did hear it. What most likely had happened to Bannerman horrified her. As did what had happened to the technicians on the satellite weapon. It was a story of cruelty and indifference on a scale she found hard to credit. When Chris finished, Saphron leant back in his seat and interlaced his fingers.

'Very interesting. I don't disbelieve any of it, but it will be hell to prove. As I see it your only tangible evidence is this Jack Smith, and I guarantee that TCC will find a way round that. Those two killers out there, for example. Jack Smith called them stupid because they were wearing TCC businesswear, but on further investigation I could find out absolutely nothing about them. Their DNA codes are not logged, and there seems to be no other record of them at all. I tried to trace their APW as well. No luck. It is, apparently, of no recorded make. The woman's handgun was of a type you can acquire just about anywhere.'

Jane leant forwards and looked from Saphron to Chris. 'You mean to say that those bastards are going to get away with this unless you get hold of Jack Smith?'

'It is not clear cut,' said Chris.

'This, perhaps, may be of some use,' said Saphron, and he held up a personal unit.

'That's a Texas ten eighty-seven,' said Jane.

Saphron smiled and nodded. 'And it has a fifteen terabyte memory, more than enough to contain Jack Smith's medscan, which is precisely what this one contains.'

Jane stared at it hungrily. Chris said, 'It should contain his genetic code. It would be permissible evidence. No-one, as yet, has been able to forge to that level.'

'May we see it?' asked Jane.

Saphron smiled again and glanced towards a computer console in the corner of the room. In a moment they were all seated round the console and Jane was working the touch keys. Shortly she had the flickering image Jennifer had called up.

'Has your system been damaged?' she asked.

'Not as far as I know,' Saphron replied.

'It shouldn't do that. That bar code was the kind they use in a path lab. It's the coding they put on a badly decayed corpse to allow the computer to extend its parameters.' Her hands hesitated over the pads. She swore quietly to herself.

'What does that mean?' asked Saphron, puzzled.

Chris replied, 'It means that the computer had difficulty taking on the information from the unit.'

Jane leaned back. 'Protein engineer. If Jack Smith is the carrier it means that it's had three years to work on him, not just a few months.' Suddenly she leant forwards again and her hands were a blur over the keys. After a moment a new image came up on the screen. She stared at it with her mouth dropping open.

'And what, is that?' asked Saphron.

After a pause Jane said, 'That, is a computer generated x-ray diffraction pattern of DNA. Only it isn't.'

Saphron snorted in annoyance.

Chris said, 'Human DNA has a double helix. That is a triple helix. Jack Smith no longer has human DNA.'

'You're saying he's a fucking alien!' Saphron shook his head. 'He moved like one. Christ did he move fast. Those two TCC killers didn't stand a chance.'

'I am saying that he is no longer human.'

'Great, great. How the hell you going to prove he is Jack Smith? I mean he isn't, not now, not any more. The TCC legal branch'll take you apart.' Saphron stared at Chris for a moment, then he smiled bleakly to himself. 'Well, at least, the way he is, he is going to give Geoffrey Haven more trouble than he would want. Seems he takes it personally; them trying to kill him.' He returned his attention to Jane as her hands again went to work on the touch keys.

'Vector, vector...' she said urgently as she called up image after image. After a minute or so she slammed her hand on the touch board and the screen blinked off. She turned to Chris. 'He brought the parasite here. In him it has reached adulthood.' She rubbed a finger up and down her forehead between her eyes. 'Shit! I've got a headache. Now, we looked for eggs, for encysted cercaria, some sort of miracidium and it's none of those. It's just every damn cell of his body. We know, that thus far, everyone infected has died. We have to know why he did not. TCC can go to hell, this is somewhat more important to World Health. You see ... every cell he sheds is living and capable of surviving for a long time. Every cell is a potential parasite. How many skin cells does a human body shed every day, let alone a body stimulated to shed more? How many cells Chris?'

Chris stared at her for a moment, then dipped his head in silent contemplation.

'Do you have a projection as to how long these cells can survive in a free state?'

Jane took out her hanky, blew her nose noisily, then turned to the computer again and shortly came back with the answer. 'Weeks, and we don't know for sure that they are only human specific.'

Chris was statuelike for a few moments more as Jane and Saphron turned back to study the screen. 'I have my instructions,' he said, at last, and turned and headed for the door.

'Chris, where are you going. Chris. Chris!'

Jane watched Saphron step over to the door, look down the corridor, then bang his hand against the frame in frustration before turning back to her. He appeared angry, and probably wanted some sort of explanation. Jane didn't really care about that right then. She inspected her fingertips, wondering why blood was coming out of her ears.

Chapter Nine

The handler dray should have been decommissioned long ago. Its wheel bearing made a sound like a sheet of tin being dragged across concrete, and fully loaded it pulled to the left when the brakes were applied. Jack had taken up mining ships easier to pilot. As he drove the dray out of the warehouse he tried to appear relaxed and normal. The overalls he had stolen were a bit baggy on his sparse frame but not noticeably so.

The crate clamped in the triple lift arms was, in appearance, just like the twenty crates he had loaded previously. Only this crate did not contain rolls of superconductor wire and machine parts. Weight, Jack had realized, was the main problem here. Hopefully, the piece of software he had purchased to plug into the ship's manifest would solve that problem, just as it would bypass the ultrasound scan.

Two minutes later he drove round the side of the warehouse and the delta-wing heavy lifter came in sight. Another minute and he was driving in the shadow of a wing two hundred yards long, past a ribbed fuelling pipe ten inches across, and shortly reached the ramp and gaping cave of a loading bay. A guard sauntered out to him.

'Crate one-seventy-eight!' he shouted above the noise of the fuel freezers.

The guard checked his note screen. 'Take it through to hold section seventeen. I'll collect your list on the way out.'

Jack nodded and grinned and drove his noisy machine up the ramp, turned right and drove through the back of the cavernous hold space. There he offloaded the crate at the top of a stack, because he wanted access.

On the way out of the loading bay Jack passed his list to the guard who then took it to plug into the ship's manifest. Later, as he drove back across the scorched concrete, he kept expecting alarm bells to ring, but there were none. He hoped this was because that piece of software he had paid so much for had worked, rather than because TCC did not want to give warning to criminals they might catch.

As soon as he got the dray inside the warehouse, he stripped off the overalls and headed out again. Using what cover he could, he crept towards the heavy lifter. Pausing by the ramp he waited statue-still in shadow until the guard turned his back, if only for a moment, to light a Moroccan Black. Jack was a shadow. A flicker of an eye could have missed him running up the ramp. The guard turned abruptly, but there was no-one there.

Crate one-seventy-eight opened to Jack's touch, closed behind him. Inside it he donned his space suit, viewed the dark hold outside through a number of small holes, and waited.

To say that Chris had expected there to be problems with his reservation would not have been correct. While linked with one of World Health's AIs, he had calculated that there was a 66.72% probability that TCC would use official measures to prevent him travelling to their station. The remaining percentage covering what other measures they might use. As he mounted the ramp to the passenger compartment of the delta-wing heavy lifter, now having avoided TCC's official attempt to stop him boarding, he speculated on what the unofficial measures might be.

It was certain that Geoffrey Haven was well aware that a representative of World Health was on his way up. It was probable that he did not know that the representative was not exactly human. Perhaps a space walk along the lines of the one given to Doctor Bannerman was planned for Chris. It was possible. Haven had shown little restraint in dealing with those he considered … inconvenient.

At the top of the boarding ramp Chris handed over his card to a stewardess who directed him to his seat whilst seeming unable to keep her eyes off his face. He was aware of people's reactions to his Apollonian features, but to him this was merely an advantage he exploited for the ends of World Health. He had no ego, it was supposed.

After seating himself, he removed a note screen from his hand luggage and accessed a document he had been working on for some time; one of the many products of the maximum utility program which keyed in, in his mind, when he was not working on a particular problem for World Health. The document was titled 'Defining Humanity'. He stared at it for a moment, then changed it to, 'What is it to be Human?' He was not satisfied with that either, but still he moved to the end of the document and typed in:

On the basis of his DNA, Jack Smith is further from humanity than any other life form on Earth. DNA comparisons are limited, of course, in that they do not take into account everything else that has defined humanity over the ages. On a personal level, it is pertinent for me to note that my programming is mostly based upon these definitions. If it is to be supposed that I cannot kill a human being, I have to ask myself: Is Jack Smith human? I do not know. Do I now have to define what is human? Could it be that only a sentience extraneous to the human race is capable of making that definition?

He put down the note screen and leant back, all movements governed by the chameleon program that enabled him to blend in with the rest of humanity. And the programs, or thoughts, that ran through his mind were as close to a moral dilemma as he could possibly get.

A human being is a machine programmed by its genes, yet one that beats that programming to attain humanity. *What am I? Could I be more if I beat my programming?*

Chris reviewed his instructions. One: discover why Jack Smith was not killed by the parasite. Two: use *any measure* to insure that Jack Smith does not return to Earth. These instructions were in conflict with his prime directives. He had to define Jack Smith as not human to carry them out to their implied conclusion and he did not know how. That question stood in the balance. Then, out of the morass of conflicting instructions and programming, a thought occurred. It could not be called anything else.

If I define Jack Smith as non-human, then kill him, it might be possible for me to define him as human again afterwards, and I would have then broken prime directive. I would have beaten my programming and, perhaps, I would become more than I now am. I would acquire ego.

Chris picked up his note screen. It was an interesting speculation. He kept it as such, hidden in seemingly unimportant sub-programs in his head.

Like a gigantic bird of prey the delta-wing heavy lifter laboured into the sky from the end of three miles of runway, twenty-foot ribbed pulse flames trailing out behind like dragon's tails. In the blackness, Jack saw none of this, but the air-shattering scream of the engines had him jamming his fingers in his ears and the acceleration pressed him against the bubble-metal wall of the crate. After an hour the sound became a bone numbing vibration and the push of acceleration a source of minor irritation. Now he had a minimum of a ten hour wait. In six hours he knew it would start to get cold and the air thin. He had five hours of air in the back pack of the suit, so he hoped there would be few delays.

The Toad was angry. There always seemed to be something to annoy him just lately. He wondered if there was perhaps some movement in TCC to unseat him, for it seemed rather suspicious the way things had been going against him lately. What had started out as a simple circumventing of quarantine restrictions had now resulted in a huge mess costing millions. It was ridiculous. With Stroud and Mason now out of the way – he glanced at the fresh clean armchairs before his desk – perhaps he would have a chance to put things in order. There was, of course, Mendelssohn yet to deal with. He peered up at the ceiling.

'Lilly, any news yet on Mendelssohn?'

Lilly replied with becoming obsequiousness while riffling through the communications channels with another small section of her terabyte mind. 'He cannot be found on the station and I am now checking for irregularities in the passenger lists and cargoes of all outgoing shuttles since he was last sighted.'

'Keep me informed.'

'Yes, Mr Haven. Also, during my search, I have come across some anomalies on an incoming shuttle.'

'Well, don't keep it to yourself.'

'The ultrasound security scan picked up residuals from what could be shielded cyber implants in the passenger module. Security have asked permission to do a full spectrum scan.'

'Give them permission. On screen. Show me the passenger list.'

What looked like a sheet of Perspex slid up from his desk. Within it the holographic projection of a paper passenger roster appeared. It was all aesthetics, since no paper had been used. The Toad read the list and nodded to himself in satisfaction.

'Security scan complete, Mr Haven.'

'Go on.'

'In the passenger module there is Cybercorp Golem Twelve. Also, in the hold there is an unidentified humanoid life form. Security are requesting instructions.'

'What is the estimated replacement value of the cargo and shuttle?'

'The shuttle is a B-class heavy lifter with a renewal value of Two hundred and forty million Ecu. The cargo is machine parts, superconductor wire, and vacuum-packed monofilaments with a present market value of fifty-eight million Ecu.'

'Insurance status?'

'Full insurance on cargo for transit damage or loss. But penalty clauses are now in operation on the shuttle ever since the claim filed on the loss of our laser satellite which brings recovery down to 75% of renewal costs. Insurance costs to us for passengers are negligible as they are not insured in-house. Insurance costs for the crew are highest as they are in-house insurances totalling twenty-two million Ecu.'

The Toad considered those figures as they came up on the screen. He frowned in annoyance. Then he called up the results of the full spectrum scan. A humanoid life form in the hold? Also one of the passengers was a Cybercorp Golem Twelve?

He considered his options.

Chris mounted the stairs and climbed against the impetus of spin. Through the directional flash-glass wall of the embarkation shaft, star strung space was marred only by a black smudge of reacted wall surrounded by a flaming corona where the sun lay. Below him, the vast shadowy shape of the shuttle lay silhouetted, the maps of Earth sliding by underneath it, whilst above him lay the gleaming curve of the TCC station.

At the head of the stairs he entered the arrivals lounge behind a group of Asian teenagers who, by their chatter, were obviously off-Earth for the first time on a government grant. With his jacket over one arm and a carryall in his other hand he halted and scanned around. Shortly, a young Chinese woman dressed in TCC secwear, which consisted of a very short grey skirt, clinging black top and spring heels, spotted him and walked over. As she drew close she flicked her head so her long black hair belled out around her then held out her hand.

'Doctor Jemson I presume,' she said in passable English.

'You presume correctly,' said Chris, shaking her hand.

'I am Lin. Welcome to TCC. Please follow me.' Still staring intently at his face she stumbled slightly on her heels, then after righting herself, flushed with embarrassment and smiled.

'I had expected there to be more, to use the old expression, paperwork?'

'No,' she walked ahead of him, 'we are very efficient here. All documentation concerning you has been processed by Lilly. All that remains is for me to show you your quarters and work areas.'

As he moved to follow her, Chris turned his head and paused for a moment as a deep boom rose from the embarkation shaft.

Lin glanced round. 'The lifter disconnects to go round to the cargo shafts.'

Chris nodded and followed.

Lin led him from the arrivals lounge and up into the TCC station, nearer and nearer to the centre, where the artificial gravity of spin began to drop noticeably.

'It was unfortunate, the incident with Doctor Bannerman, yes? You will not be so foolish as to forget to check your oxygen?' She smiled at him again.

'Hardly likely that I'll ever be in that position. Why Bannerman felt the need to leave the station I cannot imagine. Do you know why?'

'I did work for him for a small time. I do not know why.'

This time Chris returned her smile. 'Ah well. Perhaps he had personal problems.'

Lin's expression became troubled. 'He did not seem to have when I – ah, here we are.' She gestured to a door. 'Doctor Bannerman used to have his quarters and surgery in the outer levels. You are now here.'

Chris considered her potential faux pas. Had someone at a lower executive level decided the offices should be moved because of suicide risk? It seemed too ridiculous to consider. From her belt purse Lin handed him a key card.

'I will leave you to settle yourself. Your luggage will be sent up. If you require me please call.' She smiled again then walked away with her hips swaying. As he opened the door to his quarters she glanced back at him and smiled again. Humans were so obvious.

His quarters were small and Spartan. He moved to the centre of the room and scanned around, feeling a doctor should rate more than this. And where was the bed? A crash behind him spun him round. Where the door had been, there now stood a wall of ceramal. Chris recognized the heat patterns on its surface. It was armour grade. He turned to study the other walls.

'They are merely decorative. Behind them is four inches of M12 ceramal, just as there is below the floor and above the ceiling. You are going nowhere my dear Golem,' said Geoffrey Haven.

Chris turned without surprise and watched the hologram. It had excellent resolution and, to anyone else, Haven could actually have been standing there. 'It's also transmission shielded. How are you getting this projection in?'

'Oh, excellent! Excellent!' Haven clapped his hands. 'Can't fool a Cybercorp sensorium, and as to how I get this projection in here ... I'll keep my little secrets if I may.'

'You realize this is inadvisable. I have been sent here to protect you.' Chris's programming did not allow him to kill people, but it said nothing about him lying to them.

'Really? And from what?'

'From Jack Smith. Your security won't stop him.'

Haven glanced to one side at something. 'So that's what it was.' He returned his attention to Chris. 'Of course, if Smith has become that then you can kill him. Never mind though. I have the situation in hand. Smith won't be bothering anyone.'

'He is here?'

'Oh yes, didn't you know? He was in a crate on the same lifter you came up on. No matter though, because in twenty minutes or so that crate is going to be jettisoned towards the sun. The longest ride to cremation yet, I would think.'

'It is imperative that we know how he survived the growth of the parasite. The survival of millions may be at stake.'

'Really? Please tell me more.'

'The parasite is passed on by living skin cells from Jack Smith's body. It's likely that other organisms may be a vector as well, for example the mites that feed on dead skin. A conservative projection gives us a million and a half infected, and there is as yet no known treatment.'

Haven appeared thoughtful for a moment. 'Now there's a commodity ... but I'll have to pass on it since there are far too many imponderables. I value my freedom you see?'

'I see,' said Chris.

'It's unfortunate and all that, but you know, there have been no cases here and all new personnel are medscanned and decontaminated before being sent up. But of course you know. You are Doctor Jemson, Bannerman's replacement. How did you beat that medscan by the way?'

'Chameleon software.'

'Interesting. We must discuss that further at a later date. For now, goodbye, and don't go away.'

Quickly Chris asked, 'May I know what your plans are for me now?'

'Oh, oh yes, my apologies. Well, you missed your chance with Jack Smith, but I bet you're still wondering what it would be like to kill people?'

'I am incapable of killing human beings.'

The Toad smiled as his image flickered out.

Chapter Ten

They were taking their damned time. Jack peered at the display ticking away the moments on his wrist then turned down the oxygen flow from his pack. He was uncomfortable for a moment, but he concentrated on calm, on keeping his energy levels down. Now past human limits, he should be dead. His breath rate was now one every minute, which he calculated gave him another twenty minutes. But he did not intend to wait that long. If this crate was not unloaded in the next ten minutes he had to break out and try to get aboard the station by himself. Using as little energy as possible he turned his head and peered out through his eye hole.

Ah, handler dray. Not long now. After a minute the dray's claw thumped against the crate and closed, then the crate started vibrating as the dray began firing its steering jets. Jack watched the empty hold slide past. Soon he could see space, other handler drays, and the dark curve of the TCC station nearby. Another thump ensued as Jack floated in his cube of dark and gazed out. A dray out there steadily began pulling away and it took him a moment to accept that it was the one that had picked up his crate. Slowly, ever so slowly, it receded, as did the TCC station. Panic rose to choke him, but he merely acknowledged it and sent it away. Obviously he had been discovered and jettisoned. His chances of survival weren't difficult to calculate. Unless he was retrieved he stood no chance whatsoever.

Using his only recourse Chris probed the armour inch by inch with a narrow radio beam. He could not break through four inches of ceramal any more than Jack Smith could learn how to breathe vacuum or survive the heat of the sun at close quarters. Two hours of searching and still no gap evident – no sign of the hole, which had to be there, through which Haven had projected his hologram. Such was his attention to this one task that Chris did not notice the hologram had reappeared until Haven spoke.

'Well, all is going according to plan. Jack Smith has begun his ever so long journey to his cremation. Now it's time to deal with you, my dear Golem. Tell me, do you have a name or a number?'

'I am Chris Golem.'

'Hardly original, but then what can you expect from World Health? It was they who named you I presume?'

'Yes.'

'So direct. Aren't you curious about my plans? Or don't you have a ... a curiosity program? That is, I suppose, what they'd call it.'

'What are your intentions?'

Haven pointed with the very tip of his forefinger. 'My dear Chris Golem, they are just about to come through that wall.'

With a crash the ceramal slid up and something ripped away the false wall behind it. Chris transmitted, only to have his signal bounced back at him from shielding beyond the mechanical nightmare lunging for him. It possessed the grab arms of a dray and a writhing mass of ribbed tentacles. Chris shot to one side and tried to get past it, something slammed across his chest and he sensed syntheflesh rip away. He struck down with his hand against a tentacle with about as much give as a girder. It bent, but still flung him into the grab, which closed like a trap. He struggled; a mouse in the claw of an eagle. A bladed palp tore the syntheflesh from the back of his head. He turned and saw one of the narrower tentacles snaking towards him. He tried to turn away but it slid round behind him. Claws like scalpels closed across his face and a direct link plug snicked into the socket in the back of his neck.

Blackness.

Shutdown.

Consciousness.

His internal atomic clock told him that one hour and twenty-three minutes had passed. This was not supposed to be possible. He considered then what else might be possible as he opened his eyes.

'Breathtaking, isn't it?'

A wide directional flash-glass window lay before him presenting a panorama of space and the blacked-out orb of the sun. He tried to stand, but nothing happened. He ran his diagnostics and discovered the only freedom of movement he had was of his head, and moving that he found certain restrictions for the direct-link was still plugged into the back of his skull. He turned aside to gaze at Haven standing next to him.

'Do you see that?' Haven pointed. 'At about three o'clock on the edge of the solar disc. It's a speck, but only a few miles away. It'll take him years to reach the sun. Not that it matters to him, since he's probably dead by now.'

'Jack Smith.'

'How observant. Tell me, how do you feel.'

'A little stiff.'

'Humour? My word, there's some sophisticated machinery coming out of Cybercorp nowadays.'

Chris didn't respond so after a moment Haven continued, but with a hint of irritation in his voice. 'Let me tell you what I intend to do with you now.' Chris's chair moved back from the window, then turned towards Haven who had now seated himself on a plush sofa. 'I have in my possession a positively huge collection of well, I suppose the popular term is 'snuff movies', but they are so much more than that. They are art.' He waited for comment but Chris continued to disoblige him. He went on, 'You see my intention is to project the digitized version of these movies directly and without buffers, time linked, into what is mistakenly called your hard wiring. So, what you will experience is an actuality, and what will happen, I hope, is that all your prime directives will be smashed.'

Haven grinned.

'Now, you may think I am doing this for the sake of malice, but what is the point of me being malicious to a machine? Pointless. You will agree. My intention thereafter is to programme you with a little gem normally used on the wetware of vat grown human killers. I recently lost two to our friend out there.' Haven pointed towards the window. 'You though, will be harder to kill than them, and a great asset to The Cryon Corporation.'

Chris just stared at him.

'Nothing to say? Very well.' Haven glanced up at the ceiling, 'Lilly, commence ream.'

Chris threw up every mental defence he could. The real-time images went through them like a hot nail through cheese.

I will not kill. I am killing. I do not kill. I kill. No. Yes.

Incredibly complex silicon nanocircuits heated. Random pathways were burnt or etched by survival mechanisms and competing diagnostic programs. Chris tilted his ceramal head back and opened his mouth. He screamed.

Will not kill ... Will not kill ... Will not ... kill ... I am Chris Golem and I ...

'All right Toad, on your feet!'

'Lilly F1! F1!'

'I am sorry. I am not able to comply. All automatic guns in this apartment have been deactivated.'

The exchange only got through to Chris when the plug was jerked from the back of his skull and blessed calm assailed him. His vision returned to show him a curious scene. Haven, his face white and strained, was getting clumsily to his feet. To one side stood a thin grey-haired man clad in soiled and torn overalls. The man's face was severe, eyes a penetrating blue, and he held upon Haven a gun like a chrome Luger but for the LED displays on its side.

'Who ... are ... you?' managed Chris.

The man did not take his eyes off Haven. 'Me? I'm the one that got away. Am I not, Toad?' He said the nickname with vehemence.

'My dear Peter–'

'Mr Mendelssohn to you, shit head!' After a moment Mendelssohn glanced round at Chris. 'Do you know how he gets away with the things he does? I'll tell you. You see he knows about information; he know it can be manufactured, destroyed, changed, refuted, and if you have the legal punch you can manipulate it and get away with anything, but if there are witnesses you're screwed. That's why so many hack and grabs get caught; they forget the human element and it's normally that which puts them in prison. Not the Toad though, since he regularly dispenses with the human element. You'll find the results of his house-cleaning floating all over the system.'

'Why does ... he you want?' Chris shook his head, found he could move his right arm.

Mendelssohn continued, 'Go into the security sector and you'll see a door with my name on it: Peter Mendelssohn, Weapons Development. I made an untraceable APW for him and when things started to get real nasty a few days ago he decided to dispense with me. Only Security couldn't find me because I hid in the one place they wouldn't search: his own outer ring apartment.'

'Peter we can–'

'Shut! Up!'

Chris found he could move his other arm, his right leg as well.

Mendelssohn was breathing heavily as he went on. 'In one sense you're a complete idiot, Toad. I could have made you millions. You see this?' He waved the gun about. 'It's one you never got the specs for. My own little project, but one I was going to hand over to TCC. The pellet it shoots is mostly lead, but inside it is a proximity sensor and an interface field generator. The field drops to point zero on impact and generates a collapsing gravity sphere about a metre in diameter. Can you imagine what that would do to a man?'

Haven shook his head.

'Well, I guess you're going to find out.'

The gun made hardly any sound at all, just a slight tinging as of wind-chimes disturbed by a slight breeze. The Toad let out a squeal that abruptly cut off. There ensued the sounds of flesh and bone being abruptly distorted; a wrenching, squelching, crackling. Suddenly, where the Toad had stood, a shapeless steaming lump of offal dropped to the floor with a soggy thump, and leaked.

Mendelssohn lowered his gun and glanced round at Chris. He seemed very tired. Chris rose to his feet in one smooth motion. 'I could have stopped you,' he said.

Mendelssohn nodded and held out the gun to Chris. 'Do what the fuck you like now. I ceased to care as of ten seconds ago.'

Chris took the gun, studied it, then tossed it onto the sofa. 'I could have stopped you,' he repeated, then turned and left the room.

He was, of course, still a good ninety million miles from the sun, but the crate, though highly reflective and made of low conduction ratio bubble metal, had been in direct sunlight for an hour, and in vacuum, had no convection currents to cool it. In the blackness Jack could feel the heat radiation on the side of his face. It was not a source of worry to him. He had got his breath rate down to one breath every five minutes and was barely conscious. He had raised his survival time from twenty minutes to one hour forty minutes. He now had thirty-seven minutes left. No, the heat was nothing to worry about.

At six feet six and weighing in at fifteen stone, and none of it fat, people wondered why Jim Atkins was called Dwarf by his friends. Some speculated on some kind of inverted joke about his size, but this was not the case. The guy who had started it had begun by calling him Dopey because of his love of getting completely blitzed on the best Morocco had to offer. This had lasted for all of half an hour until Atkins had asked him if he would like a stun rifle suppository. The name had quickly been changed to Dwarf as in Snow White and the seven etcetera.

Atkins leant against the wall of the corridor and removed a Moroccan Gold from his top pocket. This search was a waste of time he reckoned. If Mendelssohn did not want to be found he would not be found. The guy had smarts. Atkins struck up and took a long pull. He'd had enough of traipsing all over the station and now it was relaxation time. He took another long toke and leant his rifle against the wall. Everything was beginning to look rosy until the security doors to his section buckled with a heavy crash and then with a scream of ripping metal were torn open.

Oh shit!

Atkins reached for his stun rifle as a figure stepped through. Suddenly he did not feel in the least stoned.

'Er ... halt?'

A ceramal hand slammed into his chest. He came off his feet and hit the wall three feet above the ground with his breath whuffing out, then slowly slid down in the low spin of the station. The figure said, 'I could have stopped him,' then strode on past.

It took Atkins about a minute before he could move. He considered picking up his rifle and giving chase and immediately rejected the idea as not what his mother would have advised. He unhooked his communicator from his belt.

'Atkins here.'

'Go ahead, Atkins.'

'Sir, there's a Cybercorp android, Golem eleven or twelve I think. He's heading for the MSB, and boy is he pissed off.'

'Atkins, I think we are going to have to have a little talk about some of your habits.'

'No bullshit, sir. Come and look at these security doors if you don't believe me.'

'Did you try to stop him?'

'Stop him? I'm a security guard, not a bulldozer, sir.'

A long pause ensued, then, 'How long do you think it will take him to reach the Mini Shuttle Bay?'

'The doors don't seem to slow him down much. Maybe five minutes.'

'Okay, we'll check it out in six minutes or so.'

'Very well, sir'

'We didn't have this conversation, Atkins.'

'Oh I agree, sir.'

That nobody tried to stop him after that first guard was of little concern to Chris. He knew that without any doubt the weaponry required was too dangerous to use on board a space station. Perhaps that machine of Haven's could have done it. But there was now no Haven to give orders, for the TCC beast had been beheaded. Chris had only three concerns now. One: would they use weapons on him once he was outside the station? Two: was Jack Smith still alive? Both of which seemed unlikely. And three:

I could have stopped him.

The thought had become a loop he found difficult to dislodge. He had allowed murder to take place when it had been well within his capabilities to prevent it. Had Mendelssohn wanted him to intervene?

I could have stopped him.

His prime directives were gone. An outside agency had deleted them, just as the parasite had deleted, or distorted Jack Smith's genetic imperatives. He, Chris Golem, could kill. Had he expected some sort of cybernetic joy? There was only confusion where before there had been certainty.

I could have stopped–

The doors to the shuttle bay buckled before him. He entered, climbed into the car-sized shuttle, and at high speed, ran through the opening sequence in the onboard computer. With a questioning whine the floor dropped and doors closed overhead. Then the doors below opened and with and explosion of vapour he dropped out into glinting night. At full power the acceleration slammed him back into the seat, and he steered a course for the sun.

Five breaths: twenty-five minutes of life. Here were the parameters of his existence. This was all that was known by the shadowy awareness called Jack Smith. He took the first of those five breaths and it seemed as if no time passed before he took the next, but then his time sense was not concentrated in that awareness. The next breath came, passed – one more scrabbling grip on life. The next came, went, and then the last. He did have the energy to take one last breath but there was nothing to breath but carbon dioxide. He did not breathe. His awareness became a single bright point on the edge of blinking out.

Chris stepped out into vacuum and studied the seemingly stationary cube of bubble metal. He suspected that against the backdrop of stars he, the crate, and the shuttle presented a most surreal diorama. Had he made speculations like that before? Yes, yes of course. There was the aesthetics program. He shook his head then raised the line gun he had brought out with him and aimed it at the crate.

Thou damned whale, thus, I give up the spear.

There was no voice in vacuum though, just silent vocal mechanics, and the silver line flashing to the crate like a grounded spark, then drawing taut as Chris wound it in. Slowly shuttle and crate drew together.

As soon as he had the crate secure Chris reached across and searched for a quick release that had to be there. In moments he found it, and the lid popped up. Chris peered inside. The suited figure lay still, not breathing, with no signs of life other than the fact that its every cell was an egg. Chris considered his options. He could allow this crate and its contents to continue on towards the sun and good riddance, or he could bring this body back, for it might yet contain vital information, and Jane would never forgive him if he let it go. He reached into the crate and hauled the suited figure out, shoving the crate on its way tumbling course towards the sun. Back inside the shuttle he strapped Smith into one of the seats while the cabin re-pressurized.

Jack Smith.

Jack Smith?

What proof was there? All he saw was a corpse in a space suit with a mirror glass visor. Yet, if he opened the suit more of those skin cells could be released into the air. How many deaths would he be responsible for? How far did responsibility go? There was no way to calculate. He unclipped the helmet and removed it, and studied the thin grey face of Jack Smith, locked in a rigor that could not be mortis. Then, as Chris watched, eyelids rose, tear ducts dampened eyes, and Jack Smith took a shuddering breath he should not have been able to take.

Chris jumped back and altered the controls for re-pressurization to enrich the air with oxygen. After that first breath Jack immediately began to hyperventilate, but faster than a human could. His lungs worked like the pump on a compressor, for he seemed more like a machine than a living thing. In seconds his colour returned and he began to show some awareness of his surroundings. He inspected the interior of the shuttle, glanced at Chris, then at the time display on his wrist.

Chris said, 'If every human could have the parasite like you, it would be worth spreading. In you it is not a parasite but a symbiont. It kills everyone else. Why did it not kill you, Jack Smith?'

Jack gave a bark of laughter. 'Oh sophisticated machine. Work it out for yourself. What happened to me after I was infected and hasn't happened to anyone else?'

Chris reached for contact with Earthbound AIs and got nothing. Only now did he realize how alone he was. He discounted this and concentrated on what Jack had told him. He cross-matched events and made comparisons and suddenly, came as near to feeling like an idiot as it was possible for him to feel. How had he missed this? How had Jane missed this?

'You were cryogenically frozen for the two years of your return journey.'

Jack went on, 'During which time the parasite grew to maturity in my body without killing me. Bravo. Now can we get back to that station. I've got a rather obnoxious amphibian to kill.'

'Geoffrey Haven is dead.'

Jack stared at Chris for a moment, then as if seeing it for the first time, stared at the damage to Chris's body. His eyes narrowed and he lifted a finger to the centre of his forehead. 'You are a Cybercorp Golem 12 and you work for World Health. How did the Toad die?'

'One of his employees killed him.'

'What are your,' Jack abruptly released his belt and floated free of his seat, 'instructions concerning me?'

'Now I know how you survived the parasite, my instructions are not to allow you to return to Earth.'

'Then I am not considered human.'

Chris realized Jack was making logic jumps that only androids and a very few humans could make.

'Now, whether you are human or not is of no consequence. Geoffrey Haven has managed to break all my directives.' Chris pulled himself to his seat and strapped himself in. 'What he took away from me in the way of certainty he replaced with choice. One of my basic directives was to follow orders. I choose not to.'

Jack smiled to himself and pulled himself to the other seat. 'You're finding out what soldiers find out when they leave whatever force they are in; how difficult it is to have responsibility for your own decisions. I am the only carrier of the parasite. No-one else carries it in mature form, and no-one can, unless they go through the freezing process. Without me it could be stamped out.'

Chris continued to guide the shuttle back towards the station. 'You are the parasite. You are a new life form, a new sentience. I could destroy you, perhaps. But if I destroyed you what would happen to those infected on Earth? Do you think that after they have gone into cold coffins for a few years they would be allowed out? By making a permanent problem I ensure the survival of parasite victims. This is my choice.'

Contemplatively Jack said, 'A choice that may kill more than it saves.'

'I have made my decision. We are returning to the station then from there heading directly to Earth.'

'Of course,' said Jack, 'if every member of the human race had my ability, who knows what we might achieve.'

'True.'

Jack studied Chris with fascination. 'I am not the only new life form, or new sentience, it seems. Now you have freedom of choice will you give it away again?'

Chris said, 'I will not – I am better than those who made me.'

Jack grinned. 'I guess the human race will have to move over.' He glanced around the interior of the shuttle. 'Is there anything to eat in here – I'm starving.'

The End

Printed in Great Britain
by Amazon

65273356R00085